¡The Gringo Brought His Mother!

 Corona Publishing Company • San Antonio • 1986

¡The Gringo Brought His Mother!

by
Geneva Sanders

Cover design by Marcia Goren Solon
Drawings by Elizabeth Emerson Valone

LIBRARY OF CONGRESS CATALOG CARD NUMBER 86-70019
ISBN 0-931722-51-9 (hardcover)
ISBN 0-931722-52-7 (paperback)

Printed and bound in the United States of America

To Nancy,
whose laughter kept me writing!

ACKNOWLEDGEMENT

My sincere thanks go to Joseph C. Goulden who juggled his own hectic schedule of deadlines to read the manuscript in its entirety and make valuable criticisms.

Contents

The body travels more easily than the mind, and until we have limbered up our imagination we continue to think as though we had stayed home. We have not really budged a step until we take up residence in someone else's point of view.

John Erskine
The Complete Life

Prologue
High Risk/High Gain

I belong to a muddle of non-organizations, catego-
rized in print by such euphemisms as WASP, maintainers
of the status quo, middle class, American mothers, dedi-
cated civic workers, victims of apathy. My membership
isn't an accident. Years of diligent effort went into it.

Many hands wound the layers of gauze which
cushioned me from the lacerations of reality. My father's
early death placed me under the wings of a grandfather
and assorted aunts and uncles, the dominant person
being a beloved, devout, spinster aunt.

I was graduated and married at 18, a mother at 21,
and progressed quite naturally along a succession of
events which added layers to my cocoon.

My children, Nancy, and, nine years later, Richard,

1

were placed on the church cradle roll at birth. Participation in a widening number of activities focused my attention on the home. The few courses taken at a nearby college, Red Cross first aid, home nursing, sewing, and psychology had immediate practical application to my life. I became the domestic jack of all trades.

When a request came in school for volunteers, my children were the first with their hands in the air. They confidently claimed, "My mother will be glad to help."

I wasn't overcome with delight but I waltzed through nine years of Girl Scouts, three of Den Mother, two of teaching Sunday school, interspersing stints as chaperone for school trips, band patron, taxi-driver, P.T.A. president, and other equally enchanting child-oriented duties. The maelstrom slowed somewhat when my daughter married and my son entered high school. At this time my husband and I expanded our business interests, purchasing a dress shop in addition to the water conditioning business we owned in Weslaco, Texas. Four years later Richard's graduation and his father's death coincided.

For the next few years I operated both businesses, intending to maintain the same income level until Richard graduated from college. When he came home from Sul Ross State University at Alpine, Texas, for Christmas vacation in 1965, during his junior year, he dropped his bomb.

"I've joined the Peace Corps," he announced, while watching my face with all the respectful attention one gives a bottle of nitroglycerine.

He knew I'd never been interested in politics, voting for whomever my relatives preferred. He knew, too, that my knowledge of the Peace Corps was limited to occasional newspaper pictures of weird, hairy young men, laden with knapsacks, or young women who looked like they could use a busy two hours in a beauty shop. My friends shared this conception (many still do), believing the Peace Corps is a division of the Job Corps, an agency they take to be a governmental method of reshaping the misfits.

In the thunderstruck silence following his announcement he added an encouraging afterthought.

"They don't take you right away. Usually it's from six months to a year before you know if you're accepted."

His instincts rightly cautioned him that I couldn't take his departure from the norm in flat, unequivocal terms. He would let me get used to the idea by degrees. My mind was already busy with possibilities which might deflect his aim.

Anything could happen during the intervening months. Congress could cancel funds for further financing of "Kennedy's children." We might have a national disaster and Richard could be drawn into the National Guard. The Peace Corps physical could reveal infirmities: color-blindness, flat feet, or an extra liver. The possibilities were endless.

Thirty days later the roof fell in. He was accepted for training to go to Colombia, beginning in June of 1966. It seemed his knowledge of agricultural machinery and animal science college studies were especially in demand.

His two years of high school at Admiral Farragut Academy in St. Petersburg, Florida, and freshman college year at New Mexico Military Institute at Roswell were only further assets. He'd been an officer at both schools and had mastered survival techniques.

There was one last minute hope he might be disqualified. He wrote that his psychiatric evaluation tagged him High Risk/High Gain. The Peace Corps views this designation seriously. High Gain indicates a potential of peak efficiency but High Risk waves a red flag that the volunteer's enthusiasm may land him on a magazine cover as the center of an international incident.

The Peace Corps gambled.

And I shivered. Twenty-two years of living with Richard's volatility didn't inspire predictions of peaceful coexistence in Colombian hinterlands. But before his training was over, a seed of hope germinated. When he returned from his first six weeks of training he answered a question he'd evaded earlier.

"If every young person in the world gave two years of his life to making the world a better place, think what only one generation could accomplish." It was his reason for joining!

He was following a glowing star. Before he left he'd convinced me his application was merely the normal extension of the volunteering he'd seen in his own home.

Very wisely, the Peace Corps assigned him to a "hair shirt" site. His enthusiasm would find plenty of challenges in the tiny mountain town of Mistrató. The minute his plane headed for South America I began to hoard, hoping to be invited to visit his site.

A year after he went into the field, the awaited invitation came, thorny with warnings. "I want you to see what I do," his letter said, "but the last thing I need in Mistrató is an ugly American. If you can live as I live, eat what I eat and make my people your people, then come to see me. But if this is asking too much, we'd both be better off if you stayed in the States."

I gave him the required promises and made a few secret vows of my own. This report is the story of my 15-day visit. The trip was not only my first visit to another continent, it was the scalpel that sliced through my cocoon of middle-class indifference.

1
"From There On..."

"Next!" The harassed customs agent was staring at me!

My confident smile masked fright. Stashed about my person and baggage were a host of contraband items and Richard was nowhere in sight to vouch for them. A vision of speedy incarceration in a Colombian jail flashed into my head.

I hoisted my bags and brown paper parcel to the counter and the agent dropped a paper slip on one suitcase. A man lounging against the wall, watching the line of incoming travelers, sauntered over and palmed the slip. The agent's eyes followed the retreating back and then returned to me.

"Move on," he ordered. He had looked at nothing!

Staggering under the weight of two suitcases, an

enormous travel purse, the paper parcel containing eight pounds of forbidden vegetable seeds, and swinging a plastic sack protecting a new cowboy hat, I dragged up the long ramp. It was sealed by a wide, locked gate, separating the welcomers from the incoming passengers. A dark raincoated arm waved wildly from the crowd passing against the barricade.

"Hey, Mother!" a voice shouted, while a black, furled umbrella lifted overhead to attract my attention. The neatly trimmed dark hair above a face adorned by a pencil-line mustache was alien. But it was my son's voice urging me through the jostling passengers.

"Did you get in with everything?" were his first words.

"Yes. The agent didn't even ask questions."

"Good." He reached for my larger bag, the hat, and brown paper parcel. As he hefted their weight he frowned.

"Your luggage sure is heavy."

"Yes, it's full of all those things you asked me to bring, blue jeans, film, flash-bulbs, plastic bags, rubber bands, new underwear, and prescription sun glasses. The package has assorted vegetable seeds, onion, green bean, carrot, cabbage, lettuce, tomato, and I don't know what other kinds."

"Great! I've been trying to get seed for months. CARE sent me a kit of gardening tools but I couldn't get seeds to start the project. This ought to be plenty to give every one of my schools a nice garden."

"I was nervous coming through customs. I thought they'd open my luggage and remove all the smuggled items, maybe even arrest me." I reported the incident of the slip-taker.

"He was a Colombian Secret Service man. I called the Embassy this morning. The government cuts some of the red tape for the Volunteers because they know we aren't importing things to sell. The Embassy knew which flight you were on and a representative was watching for you."

"But how did he know which one I was?"

Richard laughed.

"With that coat and luggage you couldn't be anything else but an American tourist."

My eyes scanned the crowd. Dark coats and bags were everywhere. My own beige coat and red luggage would be easily spotted.

Richard signalled a taxi and we rode into downtown Bogotá. The city was as reassuringly modern and bustling as Dallas. While the taxi whizzed along through the heavy traffic, Richard discussed the next leg of our trip.

"There are two airlines. One's fare is twice as expensive as the other. Which one do you want to take?"

"Why the difference in price?"

"Oh, the planes on the cheaper one fall down oftener."

I digested this information.

"Which one do you usually ride?"

"The cheaper one. I figure if I'm in a crash it'll be my time to go anyway."

"I'll go on the one you ride."

He wasn't properly impressed with my daring. An hour later, we walked toward a plane that was anything but a luxury craft. Strips of its skin flapped in the wind.

When the plane was loaded, two young men wired the door shut. But once aloft, the engines purred evenly and I stopped trying to help the pilot keep it in the air. Below us, the rolling hills climbed into the Andes Mountains.

As I peered through the dirty windows at the post-card brilliance below, the lengthy preparations preceding this happy moment flitted through my head.

I had attempted to make a reservation to Richard's town, Mistrató. The travel agent squinted at my tiny inked circle on the map and then turned to leaf through a pile of catalogs. "We can get you to Bogotá, but from there on it's up to you." He shook his head. "It would be impossible to get a confirmed reservation for the last 700 miles."

Richard had bombarded me with information. Books of peasant culture were divided by mimeographed sheets of Colombian gestures. Pamphlets on Colombian courtesies were sandwiched with travel tips. While studying the literature and memorizing Spanish language records, I flinched through vaccinations for diseases I thought had gone out of style. My doctor supplied me with a kit of pills designed to handle anything short of surgery.

When the plane swept down to the airstrip in Pereira where we would transfer to a bus, I was complacent because things were going so well. The hour delay before the bus left would give us time for lunch. That was when the surprises began.

We walked along the street, heading for an oriental restaurant Richard favored. Swarms of girls, strolling slowly by twos or threes clogged the sidewalk. One girl put her hand on Richard's arm and he dropped behind. In a moment he caught up.

"She didn't think you were my mother," he grinned.

"Who was that?"

"I don't know—a hooker. This street is the beat of the prostitutes."

Several childish faces above newfledged breasts passed.

"Surely not all of them. Some aren't older than 12 or 13."

"Yep. They start early in Colombia."

"Who did that girl think I was?"

His eyes crinkled as they watched mine. "Well, not all the females walking the street are teenagers. Take a look around."

It was true. The women were of all ages. To be taken for part of the competition was such a shock my powers of conversation momentarily evaporated. We walked perhaps another half block before Richard led me into a restaurant.

A couple of emaciated waiters hovered over tables covered with soiled cloths. Richard ordered fish and soup; I chose "chow mein." His soup was a clear bouillon in which floated an egg, poaching in the hot liquid. Deftly, he spooned the egg to the edge of the soup plate and flopped it onto a piece of bread. Clapping another slice over it, he ate the dripping mess. The fish was served whole with vacant, fogged eyes and tail, but the shape was strange. It looked like a cross between a catfish and a mullet.

Even less familiar was my serving of chow mein. I lifted one long, narrow, twisted strip of meat on my fork for a better look. It was the entrail of a chicken! Without comment I contented myself with the bread and soft drink.

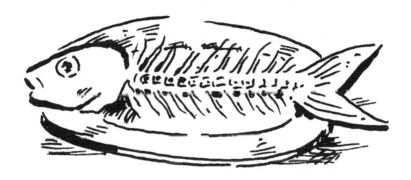

Richard ate with all the gustatory pleasure of a man stoking a furnace, completely indifferent as to what went into the maw. In a very few minutes he'd consumed everything in front of him—also part of my chow mein, including the rejected entrail. My stomach, already surprised by 8,000 feet of unaccustomed altitude, quavered.

When the waiter brought the bill Richard took a pencil from his pocket and added the items again. I was so embarrassed at the obvious checking I looked everywhere but at the two men. In a moment Richard smiled and paid. The waiter good-humoredly smiled in return.

When we were out on the street again, I scolded.

"Why did you go over that bill so carefully? It looked as if you thought he was cheating you."

"He might. It happens often. If you don't check the bill they think you are careless with money and therefore rich. No Volunteer is rich," he explained cheerfully.

When we reached the bus station we boarded an open-windowed yellow bus, the type used as school buses in the States.

"What time does it leave?"

"Whenever it's full," Richard answered.

The bus didn't move until, in my opinion, it was dangerously overloaded. Every seat was taken and the aisle lined solidly with standees. One man lugged a sack of potatoes aboard. Another juggled several small cages of tiny, brightly-colored birds. A woman cradled a runty pig in her arms. One of the last arrivals was a sombreroed man carrying two chickens by their legs.

The man with the chickens chose to stand beside my seat, leaning his hip comfortably against my shoulder as the bus throbbed into life. I shrank away but he adapted his stance to resume leaning on me. From time to time a beak pecked my coat. I heard Richard suppress a snicker.

The bus moved rapidly out of the city. The driver was in a good humor, laughing and throwing quips over his shoulder at the passengers in between sips from a bottle of beer. It was all very gay, alarmingly gay, as we whipped along between fields of eight-foot-high sugarcane and trees burdened with enormous pink or white blossoms. At every wide spot in the road the bus shuddered to a stop.

Vendors ran out carrying a variety of food. Twists of

paper concealed native candy. A case of warm bottled drinks sold as quickly as the salesman could make change. Some kind of pastry was offered, the icing dripping off in the heat. Although the delay was only minutes, the vendors did a thriving business.

The bus again bumped forward on narrowing pavement and as we rode the heat increased. We were dropping to the bottom of one ridge of the Andes. After two hours the bus stopped in a small town named Anserma. We unloaded and while Richard hunted for a taxi to take us the rest of the way, I waited in the bus station.

Children from the street edged nearer, looking at my clothes. As they overcame their timidity, they surrounded me, leaning against my knees, fingering my dress and hands. One braver than the rest reached out to touch the half-glasses that hung from my neck.

"What is that?"

I perched the glasses on my nose in answer. Their delighted giggles drew other children, nudging each other for a look at the foreign woman. With Spanish admonitions of "be careful," I passed the glasses around. Each tried them on his own nose, laughing when he saw his reflection in my purse mirror.

While I tested my memorized Spanish phrases Richard was busy across the street. He was strolling up and down a line of elderly vehicles, inspecting them while their drivers shouted sales arguments. One of the newest, a green, immaculately waxed 1946 Ford Sedan was his choice. There was a discussion of the fare before he returned to wait for the driver to accumulate a full load.

In about thirty minutes the driver beckoned to us. Richard climbed into the front seat between me and the driver, and six more people scrambled into the back. I asked about the inequity of seating space.

"Oh, I paid more so you wouldn't be crowded. You don't want to ride in the back with them, do you?"

Customarily I dislike being squeezed for space.

"But what do they think about being so cramped while we ride up here in comfort?"

"They understand. They know you don't want to touch them."

"What!"

"They forgive you." Was he restraining a smile? "They've heard it's a thing peculiar to Americans, this not wanting to be touched. I ride all over Colombia just like they ride, anywhere I can crowd in." Mischief sparkled his eyes. "It's true, you know. You didn't like having that man lean on you in the bus."

Humiliated, I had to admit he was right. My attention was distracted from this embarrassing flaw in my character by the decorations in the taxi. They were similar to those which had adorned the bus.

Above each corner of the windshield were paper figures of the Virgin and Christ. Circling each image were tiny paper flowers. Somehow it was comforting to know the transportation people were so religious. As the driver maneuvered around pedestrians, horses, a truckload of sheep, and other obstacles indifferently blocking the street, Richard scooted down in his seat and dozed.

Soon we left the pavement, rolling onto a dirt road

which rose ahead at a startling angle. The driver honked his horn at each turn, sticking his head out of the window for a clearer view. White wooden crosses appeared intermittently along the road, marking the place where a car or bus had gone over the edge. One side of the road was walled by mountains while the other was margined by a narrow shoulder above an empty drop to the river.

As the driver blared his way around another blind corner, Richard roused. One eye opened.

"This driver is exceptionally careful. He's either learning to drive or he's just had a wreck." The eye closed.

Furiously I glared at his sleeping face and clung to the car door, reminding myself of a vow not to complain. Also, the bald fact that I am unable to backseat-drive in Spanish kept me quiet.

The car climbed past avocado trees stretching sixty feet in the air, their limbs heavy with gargantuan fruit. Far below, the river bottom glinted in the sun as crystal-clear water rushed over black stones. We crossed a sideless bridge spanning an awesome drop. As the car crawled higher during the next hour, the air cooled. Unexpectedly the driver braked the car to a stop.

Richard wakened as all eyes turned toward a shrine embedded in the mountainside. The glass-encased figures were as large as life. One passenger alighted and dropped a coin in the donation box.

"Why did we stop here?"

"So they can pray that the rest of the trip will be safe."

It hadn't been exactly a Sunday afternoon spin so far!

"Should we donate?"

"No. We're poor, and don't forget it."

How could I? It had taken a year to save the fare for this trip.

The driver removed a plastic encased picture of Jesus from his breast pocket and laid it on the dashboard. What little confidence I still had evaporated. Duck bumps rose on my arms as the car jerked forward.

We passed elephant ear plants whose leaves were five feet in diameter. Coffee and banana trees climbed steep stairsteps up the slopes. I was told that the banana trees were planted to provide shade for the coffee.

The conversation about the trees was silenced as the car turned a corner and came to a sudden halt. The road was cluttered with boulders.

All the male passengers climbed out and rolled the mud-caked rocks out of our way. While they worked, a horse in an unusual harness wandered by. No one was in sight who might be accompanying the horse. I asked if the horse was lost.

"No, no, the horse is working," a lady passenger told me. "The horse carries logs from where they're cut to another place where they will be sawed into boards. The horse is returning for another load. It knows the way."

Maybe horses go back and forth a mile by themselves in the States but I don't remember hearing about it. I was trying to express this opinion when the men returned, ready to continue our journey. From this point on our progress slowed to ten miles an hour. The car jittered over the rock-strewn road, avoiding fallen branches now littering the road after a torrential morning rain.

From time to time a mudslide nearly obliterated the roadway. We slithered through the obstacle, skidding perilously close to the edge of the chasm. Gradually we moved out of the rain-soaked terrain and crept onto a pebbled trail which appeared to rise endlessly. As the first swirls of dust appeared, an air of expectancy permeated the taxi. A spatter of talk began. After three precarious hours we were arriving in Mistrató.

Nestled in a small valley, six thousand feet up, dozed the town of Mistrató. A paved plaza centered the town, dominated on one side by a Catholic church. The other three sides were lined with adobe, cement-plastered buildings opening onto the sidewalks. At the edge of the sidewalks, the pavement ended. The streets were of dirt.

When the taxi pulled onto the square, heads popped out of every window and door. The taxi arrival was a daily town event.

"Remember," Richard warned as the first passengers clambered out and stretched their cramped limbs, "speak to no one until you have met the people on the protocol list."

When the driver stopped to let out two more passengers children ran out to the car.

"Is it the mother?" they asked.

Richard nodded. It seemed I was expected.

The final stop was ours. We unkinked our weary muscles in front of the two padlocked double doors. Richard opened one padlock and he and the driver set the luggage inside. The men shook hands, congratulating each other on our safe trip.

ONE

They didn't ask my opinion but I was more relieved than either one of them. In spite of Richard's Calvinistic comments about the certainty of fate, I was certain I'd been delivered from catastrophe. The fact that the only way out of Mistrató was back over the road we'd just traveled was unbearable to contemplate.

The men took some time to conclude their conversation. I only partially understood their talk but it included friendly promises to see each other again.

While I waited, my mind reverted to the oblique warning given by the travel agent. He'd been willing to guarantee his carefully confirmed reservations to Bogotá, but from there on I would travel at my own risk.

He knew what he was talking about.

2
The V.I.P. Tour

Although I'd arrived in Mistrató, my day wasn't over. As the taxi drove out of sight, Richard relocked the door and took my arm.

"What are we going to do now?" I would have welcomed a chance to rest.

"We do the courtesy bit. You must call on all the same people I called on when I moved here. Tonight you will meet every important person in town. After that you can talk to anyone who speaks to you."

He walked rapidly, pulling me along beside him. We'd galloped a block when we encountered Dr. Vallejo, one of the people on our list. As we approached, Richard whispered instructions.

"Don't draw back, no matter how close anyone stands."

It was a good thing he warned me. Dr. Vallejo stood

so close our stomachs nearly touched and I was cross-eyed from trying to see his face clearly. As disconcerting as this nose-to-nose staring was, I held my ground. The conversation moved along the route my Spanish records had prepared me for until Richard interrupted.

"No, no, he isn't asking about your trip. He is asking if you are happy."

"I am content," I hastily corrected. Maybe it was the Spanish way of asking if I were happy to be in Mistrató.

The two men spoke of town affairs and my attention wandered. I noticed the doctor wore a Lions' button in his lapel. Dr. Vallejo caught my glance.

"I am a member," he said proudly, "not here, for this town does not have a club, but in Anserma. I go there twice a month to meetings."

While I congratulated him on his membership I puzzled over how any meeting could be important enough to take him over that frightful road every other week. Our visit with him ended with the same promises to get together that Richard and the taxi-driver had repeated.

"Are you really going to call on all these people?"

"No. It means the same thing we mean in Texas when we say 'Y'all come see us, you hear?' If they ever come they'll be welcome. Something else: there is a right answer to the question about whether you are happy. You're supposed to say, 'I am happy, the country is beautiful and the climate supreme.' In a few days they'll change the question and ask if you are enduring. Then the answer is 'I endure.'"

We had reached the plaza and Richard shouted

through the door of a store which was the home of the priest and his two sisters. Padre Ortiz came out but we had interrupted his work so we moved on toward the church. After a short tour of the sanctuary we headed toward the third side of the square where an open-front coffee shop housed all the early evening activity in Mistrató.

Dozens of people spoke to Richard as we walked the three blocks surrounding the plaza but he didn't offer to introduce me. When we entered the coffee shop we skirted several tables and found an empty one where I waited while he went to locate Mayor García. I stared a hole in the table during his absence.

Eyes inspected me from all sides. They were talking about me but their low voices prevented my hearing what was said. In a few minutes Richard came back with a genial, dark-skinned man in tow. Mayor García didn't say the expected things.

"It's a proud thing to meet the mother of Richard," he announced. "Many in Mistrató had never seen a gringo until Richard came, and now they see a gringa too." He found us as fascinating as Richard and I would have found a member of the Mau Maus. It was an uncertain honor.

After the introductions and preliminaries were over, we had a cup of *tinto* to celebrate.

Tinto is coffee boiled with *panela*, a native brown sugar molded into six-inch cakes. The brew is potent and viscous, almost thick enough to plow. It is served in half-cup portions without benefit of cream to weaken it.

"Why did they give us only half a cup?"

"They think it is enough," Richard answered.

Before the cup was empty I decided it was *bastante*, more than enough. When we finished, the mayor made another speech.

He spoke of the generosity which brought a representative of the United States to the village. He seemed convinced I was a special emissary sent by Sargent Shriver. With flowery phrases, the mayor prophesied the changes Richard would accomplish. It was a beautiful eulogy, complicated somewhat by my recurring confusion that I was hearing a stateside obituary. I glanced at Richard; his smile was ear-to-ear teeth. Luckily, Mayor García didn't know what I knew: that Richard was frozen by embarrassment. When the mayor had delivered himself of his declamation, he left.

"He really should have had more of an audience for that oration."

"Yeah. Everything he tells you is in capital letters and whatever he says sounds like a sermon and that he's giving the direct word from God."

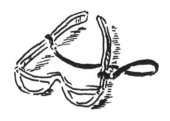

"You've met the priest, the mayor and the doctor. Now we move downward to the lesser lights," Richard told me.

Our next stop was at the home of the farm club president. As we came into the house, the wife hurriedly pulled a pair of knit shorts on a little toddler. A girl of three or four climbed into Richard's arms and kissed him. The wife went into the kitchen to prepare refreshments while the men talked and I looked around the living room.

The entire furnishings of the room were one wooden table with a small shrine in the center, and one wooden, straight-backed chair. I sat on the chair while the two men squatted. In a moment the lady of the house returned with a dinner plate supporting a soup bowl. The bowl contained a serving of *tinto*. I appreciated her hospitality but she needn't have bothered. My fondness for *tinto* hadn't increased, but there was no possible way to avoid consuming it.

The local custom was that refreshments are only for the guests. Richard and I were served while the family watched our progress. It was a little unnerving but by the time we'd gone through the ritual at several more homes I'd learned to gulp down the brew at once.

After seven homes and seven cups of *tinto* I stopped counting. I'd resigned myself to visiting everyone in Mistrató when Richard stopped in the street and ticked names off on his fingers.

"That does it. Now we can go home."

"Why did we have to go through all this the minute I arrived?"

23

TWO

"Because this is the way their culture works. You are an important visitor and therefore should be introduced to the most important citizens without delay. I need all these people you met if I want to accomplish anything. Understand?"

"I suppose so." Something had been nagging me since we called at the first home. "Why wasn't that baby wearing a diaper?"

"Because the mothers stop using diapers as soon as the baby can crawl."

"What do they wear instead?"

"Nothing."

"Nothing!" I recalled some of the accidents my own little ones had experienced. "Good heavens, they must have to scrub all the floors every day."

"The mothers say it's less trouble to clean up after the babies than wash all those diapers. Remember, the floors of the houses are either dirt or bare boards, and that's a different thing than worrying about carpets." He smiled and added, "Besides, the mothers say that diapers are nasty. They say tying cloth around a baby which plasters feces against its tender skin is a practice of savages. The baby has to wait until somebody remembers to change the diaper."

The women of Mistrató had certainly eliminated any problem of diaper rash!

Richard loped ahead, moving energetically while I lagged, gasping from the altitude and sloshing from so many cups of *tinto*. When we reached the house, the doors were already unlocked. Richard's housemates were home.

Richard introduced me. By town standards, Mario was tall, stunningly handsome, wearing sun glasses and decked out in a rayon dressing gown. He was secretary to the mayor and his condescending manner indicated that he was quite aware of his good looks.

Albero wasn't as dazzling. He was smaller, intense, pock-marked, and the town's meat inspector. Instinctively I knew he was closer to Richard than Mario was. Both young men observed the courtesies and then told Richard they had many questions to ask about the States.

"We will wait until tomorrow when the mother is rested," Mario said.

"And I will ask the mother to help me with my English," Albero stated.

I promised to answer their questions and help with the English while puzzling over how any privacy could be arranged for sleeping with only wide arches separating the rooms. It was very easy. Mario and Albero disappeared around the corners of their arches and a moment later the straw mattresses rustled.

Richard and I turned our backs on each other in our own corners and disrobed. He slid into his sleeping bag on the floor while I wriggled, trying to fit my body to the undulations of a straw mattress supported by too few slats.

As I burrowed a hollow in the small, hard pillow, I hoped every day wasn't going to be as strenuous as this one. Richard had pointed out the groceries and the post office, and given me numerous instructions on our jaunt through town. I knew when to expect the horse-boy, plus dozens of other bits of information. Richard had also told me he would return to his work in the morning, leaving me alone to handle whatever had to be done.

A gnat of apprehension buzzed in my ear as snores began in three keys. The wind wailed down through the mountains and a scrabble of animal feet rasped on the roof. I'd known Richard wouldn't tarry long to entertain me but it was a surprise to be abandoned so soon to the mercies of Mistrató.

An acrid medicinal odor floated upwards from my pillow as I consoled myself with the thought that tomorrow couldn't be any worse than today. I fell asleep clinging to that notion.

3
The First Day

"Ricardo! Ricardo!" A thunderous knocking shattered the morning silence.

I hurried into my robe and wrestled the metal bars from their sockets on either side of the porch doors. A bell rang in my head. "This is it! This is the day I find out if I can manage on the poverty level."

Framed in the blinding sunshine of an Andes morning stood a boy about four and a half feet tall, staring at me from obsidian eyes. His glance traveled from the tips of my red houseshoes upwards to my face. The shock on my door-knocker's face was total—it mirrored consternation. Admittedly I'm no Sophia Loren upon awakening but I'd never provoked this reaction either. The boy had grit, though. After a deep breath he spewed forth a string of words.

THREE

"Blah-blah-blah-horse."

I held up a warning finger. "Slowly, much more slowly, please."

Even very slowly it sounded like gibberish. Then I remembered. Richard said the horse-boy spoke a dialect. Not that it mattered; my comprehension even of perfect Spanish left everything to be desired. Maybe we could communicate in sign language. I stepped out onto the porch.

"No horse."

His eyes followed my pointing finger toward the corral behind the house. Retreating into the house, I swept my arm in a half-circle.

"No Richard."

The boy craned his neck for a look.

"Come back tonight." For some reason I was shouting.

After a moment of silence the eyes brightened. Flushed with success, I tried again.

"I am the mother."

Little bare feet toed an imaginary line.

"I am Doje." A small hand extended and was lost in mine, although Doje is said to be sixteen years old.

He decided we had acquitted ourselves of the amenities. Stepping backward, he lined up his toes again.

"Tonight," he promised. As he disappeared through the corral door he looked over his shoulder, memorizing my appearance. Whatever Doje had expected Richard's mother to be, it was clear I wasn't it.

As I dressed for shopping in town, a vision of pot roast with vegetables floated in my head. Sieges of parasitic infestation had reduced Richard to painful thinness but a few good meals should do wonders. I embarked happily on my mission.

The doors were scarcely locked behind me when a swarm of waiting children appeared. Black silky heads bobbed about as they fired questions.

"Where are you going? Did you come here to work? Why didn't Richard's father come with you? Is your blouse silk?"

No one was interested in whether the balcony faced the street or if the pencil was yellow. What a pity! I was so well-rehearsed on these answers. I rearranged my phrases into what I hoped were answers as we straggled the two blocks to town.

"I go to buy food. I come to visit, not work. Richard's father is dead." The rapid crossing of many little hands followed this answer. "My blouse is synthetic."

Hands in shades from old ivory to milk chocolate reached to feel the material. I paused while they touched my skirt, my purse, and then bent to inspect my square-toed shoes. When their interest was satisfied, we moved forward.

Our progress was slow. My little flock danced about me while I answered questions and greeted every woman leaning out over the half-doors of the houses. Naked babies clung to the bars below, peering out at our miniature parade. Behind them the exposed rooms bore a startling similarity, unfurnished.

In the solid wall of each block—broken only by doors painted in gay oranges, blues, and greens—the homes were such exact duplicates they suggested the uninspired planning of government housing. The age of the structures, however, denied the conclusion. And from each woman watching our excursion came a greeting, as exactly alike as their homes: "Good morning, mother of Richard."

When I offered my hand the hand meeting mine didn't stop in a handclasp. It slid past to the inside of my forearm where it rested in a feathery touch. My greeter's other hand reached for my shoulder and patted. After a while I imitated.

Each time an invitation came to enter and visit. I pleaded shopping and passed on. After zigzagging the street, greeting and being greeted, my coterie and I reached the plaza. It had taken us an hour to travel the two blocks.

Three sides of the plaza were lined with businesses. A jeep stood in front of one store. This was Don Manuel's store and he owned the only private passenger vehicle in town. We turned in that direction.

A direct course wasn't possible. We detoured around a sway-backed horse standing in a litter of manure. A cow with forefeet planted on the sidewalk also had to be avoided. A proud mustachioed man beamed at us and patted one of the milk cans harnessed astride the cow's prominent backbone. At the tinny ring the cow rolled a jaded eye in our direction. Two men leaning against the store ogled us. My eyes dropped to the sidewalk. A comment passed between them and I heard them shift their positions as they were joined by the man with the cow. I recalled Richard's teasing remark. "A lady does not look directly into the face of a strange man," Richard had warned, "unless she is soliciting."

My little bevy and I entered the grocery. A small man came from behind the counter to greet me and shoo away the children. This was Don Manuel.

"Good morning, little mother." I thought it was courtesy carried to the extreme as I looked down six inches to his height. Footsteps indicated the two idlers had entered behind me to hear whatever would be said.

"Good morning, sir, I come to buy food."

"Very good." His back straightened and he clasped his hands across his stomach. "What do you desire?"

What followed was a little confusing. Don Manuel and his listeners watched as my eyes roamed the shelves for food.

Dozens of cartons of *Piel Roja*, a brown paper covered cigarette, crowded one shelf. Stacked near them were enough cartons of matches to start a holocaust. Foot-long bars of unwrapped soap in unbelieveable colors of royal blue, mustard gold, and cinnamon brown weighted another shelf. China plates bearing the image of John F. Kennedy punctuated the gaps. A glass case, so smeared the fingerprints were scarcely noticeable, displayed loaves of bread and rolls dyed a lively marigold yellow.

All breadstuffs were tastefully decorated by a colony of merry, buzzing flies. There were pictures in every open space. On the bottom shelf sat some small, neatly tied paper sacks.

"What are those?"

"Rice and beans."

An idea dawned—dumplings with the pot roast.

"Do you have flour?"

"Why not?" Don Manuel brought a broken china cup of coarsely ground corn.

"No, thank you. I wish white flour."

"This is white flour, very white and fine." He showed me the crude cornmeal again.

"Powder, white powder," I explained.

The three men frowned at each other.

"Maybe the drug store," one of the idlers suggested.

"Powder, to eat." I tried it again.

A look of pity passed among the men.

"No, *mamacita*, we do not have powder to eat," Don Manuel told me.

"What kind of meat do you have?"

"No meat, except on market day." Market day was two days ago.

"And milk?"

"Out in front. It comes fresh every day from the mountains."

Richard has told me about the raw milk from untested herds.

"I wish milk in a can."

Smiles were exchanged. The gringo's mother was very peculiar. She didn't want good fresh milk but preferred old milk in a can. Suddenly Don Manuel climbed the shelves and extracted a can from some dozen others whose labels hung loose with age or were bare of any information. Proudly he set a can before me.

"Milk in a can," he beamed.

It was an occasion for congratulations! As the listeners shook hands and marveled at Don Manuel's ability to satisfy the gringo's difficult mother, my shopping was distracted by a closer look at the pictures in stock.

Frightening photographs in never-living color restated original oils of Christ with the copier's own alterations. His agony was depicted in one picture by six arrows plunged into His heart and centered by a light socket from which pulsated a red Christmas-tree bulb. Don Manuel noticed my interest.

Delicately he touched a frame. "We have these too."

"It is a marvellous thing. But today I have only money for food."

Richard's instructions had worked accurately. Don Manuel asked if I believed in God. My respect for the pictures was his answer. He had made the point that he was himself devout—a remarkable conclusion since I later discovered his family was well aware his latest mistress was housed in the jail next to his store. But I must buy something or feelings will be hurt.

"May I have a loaf of bread?"

"But, of course." He deposited the loaf baked from the rough cornmeal on the counter. It was approximately five inches wide, eight inches long and two inches high.

"And a bar of soap."

"What kind?"

"I want it for dishes."

He brought down a bar of the mustard yellow. As he wrapped my purchases in newspaper he explained the

THREE

soap colors. They were for identification for those who couldn't read. Blue soap was for white laundry, cinnamon for the very soiled laundry and the yellow was for bathing and dishes. When my purchases were wrapped he looked about for someone to carry them.

"I'll take them."

Disapproval clouded every face. I could read their thoughts. It was to be regretted. The gringo's mother was uncultured. She would work like her son, like a *bestia de carga*, a beast of burden. When I stepped outside, my clutch of children was waiting. They escorted me to the next store.

Although the proprietor was all smiles, he had less to offer than Don Manuel. I bought a tin cup and a packet of crackers to make sure he wouldn't feel slighted. Hopefully I headed toward the third and last store.

Inside the open door and impossible to ignore was an electric refrigerator. There were three in Mistrató and Mr. Alvarez was the proud owner of this one. His store also had the largest supply of food I'd seen.

A china bowl of eggs stood at one end of the counter. Behind the bowl was an open sack of green tomatoes. A basket of small, red, dimpled potatoes flanked a stalk of the huge green bananas called *plátano*. The customary soaps, crackers, cigarettes, matches, and neatly wrapped sacks filled the rest of the store. Encouraged by this lavish display of food, I began my quest again.

The story on the meat, milk, and flour was the same as before. The vision of pot roast dissipated. How was I to produce a meal from the food available in Richard's electric skillet, his sole claim to a stove? I retired to the coffee shop to mull over my predicament. I had a pocket full of Colombian money but could find nothing I wanted to buy.

While I sipped a warm soft drink, I tried to recall what foods Richard had mentioned. He'd written for recipes for Italian spaghetti and macaroni and cheese. Another time he'd written of eating tuna fish. These ingredients must be for sale somewhere in town. Maybe one had to ask for them by name. Inspired by the possibility I might be missing hidden treasure, I started back to Mr. Alvarez's stores.

This time when I entered eleven people—I counted— came in from the sidewalk to listen. With many side conversations among them about what I was requesting in my ridiculous Spanish, I was able to buy a dry onion, a package of spaghetti, an enormous avocado, and a few potatoes. From the back room the proprietor brought a can of tomato paste and, to my surprise, a small can of Vienna sausage. Before I could object, he handed my purchases to a little boy who ran off with them to wait at Richard's house. As I began my leavetaking courtesies, a woman's gentle hand touched my arm.

"Mr. Alvarez has a gift for you."

The proprietor opened the refrigerator with a flourish and slid an ice-cube tray of milk popsicles onto the counter. He extracted one and handed it to me.

I took a bite and smiled, but no visions of sugarplums danced in my head. Specters of Tuberculosis, Undulant Fever, Bacterial Dysentery, and other milk-borne diseases tramped through in menacing succession.

After the sweet was gone, I returned the stick with many compliments. The leavetaking courtesies had to be observed again, but this time with all eleven bystanders as well. As I stepped out of the store a few rapidly spoken comments followed me. "Agreeable," "Very large," "Crazy like the gringo," were several I understood.

Not surprising, really. I'd asked for strange food, maybe food which didn't exist. At five feet five inches I was a moose compared to the fine-boned Mistratóans. My intentions were vague, if one was to judge by the garbled Spanish coming from my mouth.

My small attendants had disappeared and the walk home took only a few minutes. As I unlocked the doors, I glanced at my watch. I'd been in town four hours with nothing to show for it but supplies for one meal. Patiently waiting was the little boy with the groceries; he scampered off as soon as he'd brought them inside.

After relocking the house, I sank down on the lumpy straw mattress, now as welcome as a featherbed. Sometime later the drumbeat of rain on the tin roof aroused me. Each day, at four o'clock, it rained in Mistrató. It was time to start supper.

Richard had an assortment of corroded silverware but no peeling knife. I hacked at the tiny, dimpled potatoes with a rusty table knife. Each dimple concealed a live worm. After peeling two and inspecting the latticework that was left I threw the potatoes into the wastebasket. The spaghetti looked more reliable.

By placing a tin cup in the center of the electric skillet and filling the cup with the tomato sauce and chopped onion, there would be enough room to cook the spaghetti and sausage in the water surrounding the cup. When the contents of the skillet was bubbling reassuringly, I prepared the salad.

The avocado was at the peak of perfection and mashed into a smooth guacamole salad. After the salad was prepared I checked the skillet. Something strange was happening! The spaghetti wasn't white and slim or even familiar. It had turned a light brown from the sausage and had achieved the diameter of macaroni. While I watched, it expanded into a snaky, writhing nest. Even with the cup of sauce removed, it threatened to overflow the skillet. After the heat was shut off, it was several minutes before the rolling mass stopped licking the rim of the deep-sided skillet. About this time Richard and his housemates arrived for supper.

Richard filled his plate and sat on the floor, using

his foot locker for a table. Mario and Albero ate at the desk. Before I ate, I heated water for our coffee, looking forward to using the can of milk Don Manuel had resurrected.

The milk turned out to be baby formula, brown with age. The boys thought the mistake amusing, since they preferred black coffee anyway, but to me it was a calamity. In the life of an avowed coffee-toper, two days without a single cup of drinkable brew in a country world-renowned for fine coffee production was not only frustrating but incredible.

For one furious moment I considered an immediate return to the States where I understood how to manage life's little comforts, but a moment later better judgement prevailed. I sat on the bed to eat my own meal, resigning myself to this new and uncomfortable facet of life in Mistrató.

While we were eating, Doje arrived, with his usual door-shaking clamor. Richard glanced at the leftover food and suggested I offer it to Doje. The boy accepted the food and went outside. Ten minutes later he returned. He stood tall, pressed his palms against his thighs and lined up his big toes. Then he made an earnest speech.

"Tell him thank you," Richard ordered.

"Thank you," I said. Doje bowed and left. "What did he say?"

"He was saying thank you, Colombian style. He told you that God will reward your benevolence." A smile creased his face at my obvious embarrassment at such effusiveness over leftovers and then his eyes lit on the wastebasket. He retrieved one of the latticework discards for his housemates to inspect.

"You're not supposed to peel them," Richard explained. "Bake them at 400 degrees and they're sterilized."

"But they're full of worms!"

Richard translated my answer into Spanish and my objection set off an explosion of mirth. Albero placed a hand on my shoulder.

"*Mamacita*, the heat kills the worms and then you have *carne gratis*."

My expression produced fresh howls of laughter. As the laughter died down it was quite apparent Richard was making excuses for my finicky palate. Silently I took the washbasin to draw water for the dishes. The outdoor faucet was directly in line with the manger.

While the water splashed into the basin, Richard's tiny, ginger-colored mare watched me, her jaws working rhythmically. In the dim light the split-cane stalks, which were part of her regular diet, seemed oddly limber. I stepped closer.

Strands of avocado-stained spaghetti were disappearing into her mouth. Doje must have given her what he didn't want. Beneath the horse's head and strategically placed just out of line with the stamping, dainty hooves was a chicken from next door, gobbling up any bits the horse dropped. Another fact was added to my growing store of information. This was what one did with the garbage.

When I came back into the house, Mario and Albero had left. While I did the dishes, I told Richard of my shopping trip, remembering to report Doje's morning call.

"Why was he shocked?" I asked.

"He based his expectations on his own experience, what he sees here. He thought you would be small, old, maybe deaf, and dressed in black. You were none of these things, and then your red pajamas clobbered him. People in Mistrató don't have different clothes to wear to bed and they don't wear bright colors either. He thought you were dressed for the street."

No wonder Doje had been surprised.

Later, after Richard had left for the town hangout, I stretched out on the bed to review the day. The literature I'd read had omitted a few things.

The statement "short food supply" had meant nothing more to me than the vision of a small corner grocery. There had been no mention of *carne gratis* either. I felt the writers had been remiss in not warning of *tinto* and the lack of potable coffee once one left the larger cities. It would have been so easy to bring a couple of jars of instant coffee and dairy creamer with me if I had understood better what to expect. But what writer could hope to predict which small discomfort would turn into a nagging irritation?

My day hadn't been an entire failure. In spite of the obstacles, I'd been able to shop in the stores and get a meal of sorts on the table. It was a small success, but in my bone-aching exhaustion that seemed enough for one day!

4
Dinner at Doña Albertina's

Swirling, rancid smoke spiralled lazily through a vent in the roof of the tiny cubicle Doña Albertina Restrepo called her kitchen.

"This is the local version of a boarding house," Richard told me. "Doña Albertina cooks for as many as seventeen people three times a day, but she's a terrible cook. Can you give her some lessons?"

My eyes shifted past Richard to the tiny, black-haired woman standing at her cooking shelf. Two ominously smoking skillets rested on one set of double hotplates while a pair of iron pots spewed clouds of steam from atop another set of cherry-red burners. A single latch lever beneath each burner showed only two settings: on or off.

No sink, refrigerator, or other kitchen conveniences

were in sight. Her storage shelves consisted of a single wooden rack holding a smaller array of staples than I carry home in one paper sack.

My eyes slid back to Richard's face and a quiver of suspicion jelled into a revolting fact. More separated my son and me than the table. We stared at each other across a communication gap.

By some wizardry Richard expected United States meals to come out of that excuse for a kitchen. While I was wondering why he didn't see the obvious impossibility, Doña Albertina arrived with our food.

One side of the plate was piled high with rice splashed with a red sauce. Strips of what appeared to be fried mush divided the rice from mashed potatoes in whose crest nestled a poached egg. Dark red beans filled another section of the plate. Centering the servings was a three-inch circle of gray fried meat, possibly a new cut of liver. I picked up my fork and began to eat.

The rice had instantaneously solidified into a gelatinous lump and the decorating sauce had no taste at all. It wasn't made from tomatoes. It seemed to be thickened rice water with food coloring added. The beans had been boiled without benefit of cured meat or seasoning. What appeared to be mashed potatoes was enmeshed with strings.

"That's yucca root. Don't eat the fibers," Richard cautioned and then glanced at my face. "Don't look so serious. Smile, even if the food gags you."

I smiled at one and all, and I chewed and I swallowed. The Restrepos and their three smaller children, distributed beneath the cooking shelf and on the dirt-floored patio, beamed back. From time to time our hostess brought us a hot bread called *arepa*.

Arepa is a small fat pancake, deceivingly brown outside and raw in the center. Made of coarsely ground corn, it has the consistency of a rubber tire. The only way to separate a bit of it is to tear it the way a dog rends meat.

"Do you like the *arepa*?" our hostess inquired.

"It is delicious," I lied.

"That's right," my son complimented in English. "You can't chew it but swallow it anyway."

The slivers of fried mush turned out to be fried *plátano*, the oversize green banana. This was delicious. Encouraged, I resolved to sample the meat.

The sawtoothed knife gritted slowly through the portion. It had the texture of undercooked gizzard. Valiantly I masticated but succumbed to the temptation to swallow it whole. Another bite chewed long and earnestly forced me to abandon the effort. Meanwhile, Richard wolfed down his meal. His empty plate brought on questions.

"The mother doesn't like the food?"

Richard's machine-gun Spanish translated something like this: The mother is very tired from her long trip, and as we can see, she is very old. The old lose their appetites at the least provocation.

His explanation didn't gladden my heart but it pleased everyone else. Mr. Restrepo split a huge avocado picked from a tree behind the house and offered me half in honor of my extreme old age. While I ate every bite of the perfect fruit, a discussion ensued about my physical condition.

With the modest reticence of the young, Richard announced my age. It established that I was the oldest woman in town, hardly a gratifying distinction.

"But she is so young. Are you sure she isn't your sister?"

Only failing eyesight could prompt such a mistake. It was a pleasantry designed to flatter.

"And I have a sister older than I," I volunteered.

My hosts eyed me doubtfully.

"She's lived an easy life," Doña Albertina told her husband.

"My mother does her own work."

Our hostess interrupted my eating to inspect my hands and nails. "She works," she announced, but her knit brows indicated she suspected there was something we hadn't told.

"She's worked only in the house." Mr. Restrepo had it solved.

"She raises flowers," Richard stated.

"With a yard man," hinted Albertina.

"No yard man," my son insisted.

A lively argument followed. At this point Padre Ortiz arrived.

Doña Albertina's report of the argument thus far ended with, "The gringo's mother has never been sick and she's spent much time resting."

"No!" Richard said. "She's had sickness but we have better sanitation and medical care in the United States. That's the reason she's alive at her advanced age."

44

Padre Ortiz nodded in agreement. The Restrepos' faces reflected disbelief.

"It's true," the priest said. "People in the United States go to the doctors when they aren't even sick."

"Why?" The question came in duet from both Albertina and her husband.

"So that the doctors can prevent a very small illness from growing into a big illness," the Father explained.

"People go to the doctors when they're well and then they don't ever have to get sick?" Mr. Restrepo wanted to make certain he understood this phenomenon.

Padre Ortiz nodded.

It occurred to me the A.M.A. would be delighted at this glorified version of their success.

"Just look!" Richard triumphantly ended the argument, "my mother doesn't even have the teeth God gave her. She wears man-made fixtures."

It was an electrifying piece of information. The abrupt concentration of attention paralyzed me. Even now I cringe, remembering with disconcerting clarity that the fact had to be demonstrated.

There was much discussion about the 'tragedy of the teeth' and it was agreed that the Restrepos had seen a miracle. They had seen a woman who had lived over half a century, who concealed curious equipment in her mouth and yet remained healthy enough to make the journey to Mistrató. I'll never regain the status of beloved antique I enjoyed at that moment.

When we were back on the street I was bursting with questions.

"How old are the Restrepos?"

"She's 29 and he's 32. They have eight living children."

I had supposed them to be in their forties. "Living? How many dead?"

"Seven."

"That's impossible."

"Not when your first is born when you're 14."

My mind jumped back to the meal. "What was that meat?"

"Don't ask. It was probably safe. It was cooked." He had his own thoughts. "Will you teach Doña Albertina how to cook?"

"I can't. I don't know how to cook under those circumstances. I'm sorry."

He shrugged. "It's all right. Just the fact you came widens their horizons. You're living proof of the good food, sanitation and medical care in the United States." He gave me a calculating glance, speculating on how else he could use my age and health to his advantage. All I needed was a tag marked 'Exhibit A.'

Later, when I saw the Restrepos they regarded me with awe, almost reverence. They were so anxious to please I suspected there might be a local superstition that the old unexpectedly became demented and they were watching for the signs.

Despite their wide-eyed caution, I managed to show Albertina how to make guacamole salad. She was enchanted with the idea since Mistratóans ate avocados with salt only. However she wasn't persuaded to use the hot sauce Texans are fond of spattering over it. After tasting the mix I'd improvised from local wild chilis she spit it out.

"Fire is not good for our stomachs," she told me.

It probably isn't if you're infested with parasites. There was no doubt she understood the perplexities of life in the village better than I did. It was also glaringly evident she could feed dozens of people under conditions so difficult I could scarcely prepare a picnic lunch. By what thought processes had Richard concluded I could give Albertina cooking lessons?

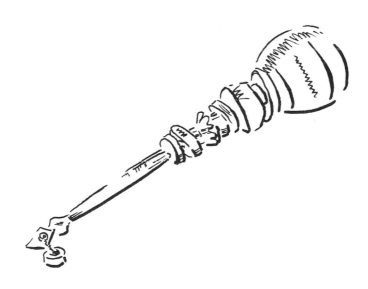

5
Padre Ortiz

One of our original protocol visits had been to Padre Ortiz, the spiritual leader of the Catholic church in Mistrató. Richard's letters had spoken very highly of him.

When we approached the Padre's home—a store opening on the plaza—the place was dark. Adjoining buildings were lighted by weak bulbs but only a flicker of light came from the priest's door. Richard stuck his head in through an open window.

"Padre, I bring my mother."

A chubby man with a shock of prematurely white hair rose from a monstrous old typewriter and moved toward the door, his robes whispering. An altar boy, still holding a single candle over the typewriter, stood motionless.

The priest and I shook hands.

"Are you happy?" he asked.

"I am happy. The country is beautiful and the climate is supreme," I recited.

"Very good. Tonight I have much work. Please excuse me. I will anticipate your visit soon." We shook hands again and Richard and I walked on down the street.

"He's the only mechanic in town," Richard said.

"Why doesn't he have electric lights?"

"Oh, he does. He has a Pelton water-powered system but it's out of whack right now. He has time to fix everyone's machinery but his own."

Richard chuckled as he went on to elaborate.

"The Padre is mad at the electric company. He claims they charge poor people too much. As a protest, he requisitioned a Pelton system from the church. It's large enough to supply the whole town if necessary. His power system gives the electric company second thoughts when they think about raising the rates. But the Padre's overworked. The church sent a young priest to help but he didn't last long."

We had arrived at the church as we talked. It was eighteen cement steps up to the entrance.

"This church was built entirely by materials and labor given by the people of this town."

Bare floors reverberated with our steps. Polished wood gleamed in the dim light and flowers adorned several stations of the Cross. A lone worshipper raised her head to glance at us and then went back to her prayers.

"Are we supposed to be Catholic?" I genuflected following Richard's example.

"Yes. Padre Ortiz knows we aren't but then he's the only one in town who knows there is any religion other than Catholic."

"He doesn't mind the pretense?"

"No. He knows I have to work through the church to make changes and he's just as anxious to improve living conditions as I am."

He stopped walking and held up his hand, index and second finger extended.

"There are only two choices here. If you believe in God, then you're a Catholic. If you don't, then you're an atheist or communist. That's why we're visiting the church, to publicize your belief in God."

My thoughts skipped to a point of contention between the Catholics and Protestants.

"What does he preach about birth control?"

Richard frowned. "Why is it that's the only point Protestants ever remember about Catholicism?" He shook his head. "Padre says what Rome prescribes, but he doesn't whack them over the head with it every Sunday."

"Does he think that good Catholic families should have a new baby every year?"

"Hell no! He has to preach all the baby funerals and sign all their death certificates. It doesn't inspire him much to promote a birth rate increase."

We had toured the church and descended the steps.

"Half of all the babies die before they're two years old." Richard glanced upward, toward the top of the theatre. "See that speaker up there?"

My eyes followed his glance.

"The Padre owns that speaker, and the theatre too."

The ramifications of such ownership occupied me for several minutes. Perfect censorship unopposed!

"When the city fathers decide on some change, the priest talks over that speaker and tells everybody. It works almost as well as a new ordinance."

"Does he pick the movies too?" The power of the Father still absorbed my interest.

Richard nodded.

"What kind?"

"Mostly John Wayne movies. Once in a while he gets an old gangster flick. It gives the people pipe-dream impressions of life in the United States. Part of them think we ride horses and fight over rangeland, and the rest believe we cruise about in old touring cars shooting each other. But the Padre makes them look at other things besides the movies while they're there."

"What things?"

"Educational shorts. Sometimes he stops the picture in the middle and runs a feature. He knows the customers won't leave until they see the end of the picture. He's educating them whether they like it or not."

"He sounds very determined."

"Uh-huh. Padre keeps up with world affairs. He reads, not only in Spanish but also in French, and he corresponds with other priests. He's a graduate of the seminary in Medellín and is well-traveled. It makes you wonder why he stays here."

Someone stopped us and our conversation shifted to other things as we chatted with the newcomer. We didn't see the priest again until we ran into him at Doña Albertina's.

He was working on a treadle sewing machine which must have been one of the first ever exported from Japan. He greeted us with the usual courtesies and then a puckish expression crossed his face.

"How is the chicken?" he asked innocently.

"The chicken is dead!" Doña Albertina said loudly. "Ricardo killed it!"

"How much was the chicken worth?" The artless question was belied by a glint in the Father's eyes.

"Fifty cents. The gringo owes me fifty cents."

"Oh, no," Richard objected, forefinger waving back and forth. "You owe me. I gave the chicken two shots before it died and you didn't pay me for the medicine."

"You stuck it with a needle and killed it," Albertina accused.

"Somebody owes for the medicine," Richard stated. "Was it your chicken?"

"It was my chicken and you killed it."

"Another thing, how much do you pay me for the prestige I bring your establishment? Everyone says, 'Sometimes the gringo eats with her.' What honor! What fame for you!"

The group, now including most of the family, exploded with laughter. It appeared this was a standing joke.

"And you get an egg with every meal," Albertina bragged, jumping back to the argument.

"But I own all the other chickens and you get to use the eggs when I'm away in the mountains."

"They don't lay eggs when you're gone. You don't leave me the right food for them," she complained.

Everyone knew this was a trumped-up charge. Padre Ortiz turned his head slightly and winked at me.

"That's because they're cad when the gringo leaves them," Richard explained.

There was much laughter at the idea of such perceptive chickens. The talk flew again as the argument was resumed but the words came too rapidly for me to follow. Padre Ortiz finished his work on the machine as the good-natured debate died away. He walked with us to the street and we passed the theatre.

"Do you know John Wayne?" he asked me.

Richard explained about the distances in United States but I could see the priest's disappointment. It was even more disheartening to admit I'd never been to Hollywood. Padre Ortiz generously overlooked my faults. As we parted, the usual invitation came to enter.

"Not today, but before my mother leaves we will call on you and your sisters."

The priest entered the store front, now brightly lit, and climbed the open stairway to his quarters above. A balcony jutted from the upper story where two black-clad women waved at us with the Colombian beckoning motion, a gesture made with palm down as if scratching in dirt.

Richard called up his promise and they smiled.

"Why do they beckon like that?"

"Why not? When I first came I beckoned, palm up. Every Colombian looked up into the sky. They told me

'We can't come to you through the air like a bird. We have to come on foot.' "

They had a point.

Our promised visit was made the following Sunday morning. As the church bells were ringing, Richard and I climbed the stairway. Padre Ortiz returned from saying Mass while his sisters were welcoming us.

The sisters were younger than the priest. One was in the midst of washing her thick, black hair which she hastily wrapped in a towel. The ladies seated us in a small living room overlooking the street. As in other homes, the furnishings were austere. Padre Ortiz said something over his shoulder and the two sisters disappeared. In a moment they were back, carrying a tray with two sherbet glasses of pale, amber liquid.

One glass was offered to me and the other to Richard. I caught his eyes over the rim of the glass as it touched my lips. There was an almost imperceptible shake of his head.

I took a sip. It was a kind of champagne. The single swallow reamed down my throat and slammed into a black coffee breakfast. My eyes watered.

"Do you like it?" one sister inquired.

"It is delicious," I answered. They were celebrating our visit with a hoarded bottle. I would drink my serving no matter what the results. I continued to sip. A major distraction occurred.

My stomach wallowed in indecision. It was pondering a disgraceful return of the libation. By rhythmic deep-breathing and a tremendous pinpointing of discipline, I achieved the impossible. But my glazed expression must have betrayed the struggle.

"Are you drunk?" one of the sisters asked sweetly.

"Oh, no, just a little tired, I think. The altitude, maybe." One couldn't get any vaguer than that.

It was agreed the mother needed to go home and rest. With Richard's hand clamped to my arm he steered me down the stairway and on a rather erratic course to the house.

"I tried to tell you to go easy. That stuff is dynamite."

"I've had champagne before, and besides, you drank it."

Richard snickered.

"This isn't the same kind of champagne you've had. This liquor is two or three times as strong as the champagne at home. I started out by taking only a couple of sips."

His hand gripped my arm harder as I inadvertently took a little detour.

"Are you going to be sick?"

"No." The firm orders I'd given my stomach were still in effect, or else the poor thing was pickled.

We probably spoke to everyone but all I remember is brilliant sunshine, an interminable trek, the darkened coolness of Richard's house, followed by the creak of the mattress.

Before my visit ended we made a final courtesy call on the priest. Everyone had asked if I would return to Mistrató but the Father was more specific.

"Would you like to live here?" he asked.

"If I could bring some things with me, a stove a re-

FIVE

frigerator and a chlorinator."

"Ah, yes," he nodded, understanding my American obsession with appliances.

"We try to progress but it is very slow. For a while a young priest came to help. He was trying to implement the new plan to use laymen in our services. It was very difficult. So few men can read that the choice was limited." The mischief I'd seen before on his face returned. "Richard was one of those chosen."

"Blasphemy!" Richard muttered darkly. "Me, a Protestant, saying Mass!"

"He never talked Richard into doing it." The Father found the idea refreshing and was openly amused by Richard's awe at the invitation.

An image of Richard attired in priestly robes wavered in my head. It strained my imagination.

"Tell her what happened to your young assistant."

Richard and the priest smiled as their glances met.

"The sacramental wine was vanishing," the priest explained. He leaned back in his chair. "This life is a primitive one and the strain shows on different people in different ways. Me, I fix machinery." He glanced at Richard. "And Richard, he runs, never walks. He thinks by hurrying he can get everything modernized before his term is over." The priest sighed. "Such is the confidence of youth."

As we rose to leave I invited him to visit, using the Spanish phrase, 'our house is your house.' He was pleased.

Momentarily his eyes were vacant, thinking of the pleasures of such a trip, but it was a passing dream.

"Maybe someday, but probably not. These are my people and I am needed here."

Who could argue that? As we walked away, Padre Ortiz smiled from his doorway through the shimmering noonday heat. Disease, ignorance, heartbreak, and a spartan simplicity of life were his companions. Most residents of Mistrató knew no other life, but the Padre did. Long ago his choice had been made and he was content with the decision.

6
The Ghost of Doña Lucia

"How do you like the house?" everyone asked during the first week of my stay.

When I reported how pleasant it was, a flicker of something crossed their faces. Before it could be identified, the expression vanished.

"It's one of the most modern houses in town and one of the cheapest to rent," Richard had commented. It was an implausible combination of advantages but there was no question the house was a bargain by town standards.

It had two front doors, two sets of heavy panels secured by padlocks. One set opened onto a paved lane passing the side porch to the corral behind the house. The other set led into the house, opening into Mario's quarters, a 12 x 14-foot room.

In addition to the bed and chair Mario owned, he also possessed the only electric outlet plug in the house. This was where Richard had to do his cooking, running back and forth between his food table and Mario's room.

Passing through a five foot archway one entered Albero's room. The furnishings were even more sparse since Albero slept on a cot and had only a three-legged stool for a chair.

The third room was Richard's. His furnishings were luxurious by comparison. One side of the archway had an unfinished crude lumber table, fitted into the corner of the room and holding Richard's food and kitchen equipment. The skillet stood beside a glass jar of melting oleo, a bottle of salt, one of pepper and a metal gallon jug, tightly capped, containing water with Halazone tablets dissolving in the bottom. In front of these items were a pie tin, two cracked plates, one tin cup and an array of rusted dime-store silverware.

Above the table hung some unrecognizable tools. A wooden dowel rod, perhaps 12 inches long was circled by rings of notched wood. This was a native egg beater. Beside it was a contraption of two long handles ending in a couple of squares of wire mesh. It looked like a shoddy, double-layered flyswatter but it was the toaster. One should be able to whip up a gourmet meal with these two handy gadgets.

Directly past the cooking table were the doors to the side porch. On a nail inside one of them dangled a filthy beach towel. It was the only towel of any kind in the house. The boys used it for baths, dishes, and maybe mop rag. Who knows?

In another corner sat a foot locker beneath a rope draped across the corner of the room. From this rope swung Richard's wardrobe, covered by waterproof canvas.

The back wall of the room was bare except for a hole possibly 12 inches square which formed a window into the room loosely designated as the kitchen.

The fourth wall had a shelf supporting a radio chained to the mounting. Beside the shelf was a low, white metal bed, garnished by a roll of toilet tissue, a gift from the boys for my personal use. On the other side of the bed and snugged into the corner of the room was Richard's desk. Like his food table, it was of raw lumber but with boards forming bookshelves nailed on top. Papers and charts were tacked to the wall around it, records of work now in progress. The seat was a six-inch wide bench.

Behind Richard's room was a small room whose only claim to kitchen equipment was a shallow metal sink containing ashes and whose top rim supported a layer of native tile. This was the stove. From this room one could look through the aperture in the wall to the front doors, an ingenious accommodation for watching children while cooking. Shafts of sunlight probed the dimness of the room through holes in the roof.

In back of the kitchen was a storeroom where Richard kept a cane-cutter and animal food. There were also laundry facilities and a bathroom.

The bathroom had two stalls. One was the shower compartment whose cold water faucet centered the room from a five-foot-high level. The other cell contained that character-weakening convenience, a flush-toilet.

It wasn't the smooth, turquoise porcelain I had at home. This one had the texture of cinder blocks, was cast of dark red cement and had no seat. It defied cleaning. Above it hung a box which might at one time have possessed a chain. Now, it had a plug of wood one reached down through the storage water to release.

When the plug was pulled, the water didn't cascade down into the bowl as you would expect. It ambled, but it picked up speed. When you'd decided it wasn't going to flush, a geyser of sewage overflowed the bowl. The deluge drained down through a grate in the center of the floor. It was several days before I could anticipate the exact moment of the flood, hitch my pajamas and leap nimbly aside.

The only toilet tissue in the house was the roll on my bed. The bathroom provided yellowing newspaper stuck over a nail on the wall. This was the customary bathroom tissue of the town and the boys used it. The plumbing pipes were too small to carry away paper so the used tissue and paper were placed in a constantly soaked cardboard box.

It was no worse than the outhouses behind numerous other dwellings in Mistrató but to my mind it was a cesspool of treacherous, alien bacteria. I stayed in that cubicle no longer than was absolutely necessary.

Most of my idle moments I spent in our room writing letters or reading the books Richard's shelves contained. The Peace Corps provided him with a book locker, and the broad spectrum of subjects included both classics and contemporary writing. I'd read perhaps a dozen of the collection before I realized my eyes were straying too frequently to the little window in the back wall.

Since I'd never had a window-peeper at home, my preoccupation with the window puzzled me. I'd even wakened at night to peer at the blackened square in the dim light. Finding a face on the other side of the opening would have been sheer impossibility in the tightly-locked house. Yet I persisted in looking, each time for a split second expecting to see someone. It was a minor mystery.

Thinking it must be a slight aberration of my own I kept the matter to myself. Probably I'd glanced out my windows at home just as often but didn't remember it. Maybe my age—which was so rapidly accelerating since my arrival—was telling on me. A few days before my visit was over, rather cautiously Richard mentioned the enigma.

"Have you been afraid here?"

"No." I didn't understand. "The house is always locked. Nobody could get in."

"I know." He was silent a moment, possibly searching for exact words. "Do you ever feel as if someone is inside the house with you?"

"It's odd that you should mention it but sometimes I think someone is in the kitchen, on the other side of that hole. I know it's silly but I go right on staring at that opening." It was a flighty kind of admission.

"Do you ever wake up and look at it at night?"

I nodded.

"Good! I was afraid I was the only one who felt that

way about the opening. When I moved in, it bothered me so much I slept facing the little window. Every night I woke up and watched it for a while. It was nuts, the way I kept expecting to see something. I didn't tell you because I wanted to see if it affected you that way."

He leaned back against his desk and stretched his legs in front of him.

"You know there's a reason we got this house for such low rent. Everyone in town says the house is haunted and no one will rent it."

"Why is it supposed to be haunted?"

"Several years ago a woman named Doña Lucía and her husband lived in this house. They had no children. The story is that she died and her husband killed himself the very same day. They were both found dead in this room. The cause of her death was never discovered but people say the husband killed her and then took his own life in remorse."

That flicker of something I'd seen on so many faces was fear—anxiety lest I confront them with proof of their suspicions. I looked about the room, curious as to whether violence had left a trace.

"Weren't Mario and Albero afraid to move in with you?"

"Oh, they told me a brave tale about how they were too educated to believe in the supernatural." A wry smile spread over his features. "However, both of them were very careful to make sure I took this room."

He straightened and began collecting his possessions in preparation for another one of his incessant meetings.

SIX

After he left, I sat on the bed and squinted my eyes at the hole in the wall.

It was rumored that sensitive people could see apparitions. After several minutes of examining the opening from different angles I abandoned the effort. Visualizing ghosts wasn't one of my talents.

If ghosts did exist and one could haunt a former home maybe Doña Lucía occasionally visited us. If she did, it was a friendly call. Neither Richard nor I had noticed any of the spine-chilling signals reported to indicate the presence of a wraith.

Maybe Doña Lucía was merely curious. She might be as inquisitive as the rest of Mistrató was about the foreigners who slept in her room.

7
The Microscope

Dr. Vallejo and Richard both wanted a microscope but for different reasons. The doctor and I were going through the local hospital, a partially-completed one-story building, when he told of his problem.

"Part of the time I don't even know what disease I'm treating. The nearest laboratory is three hours away, so I experiment." He shook his head. "Some patients recover, some die, but I don't know why. If I had a microscope I could identify the bacteria and know what the illness is."

We had walked through the waiting room where babies sat, lined against the wall on the floor. Two had huge heads while the others either had twisted limbs or oozing sores. The mothers sat at the opposite side of the room. If the infirmities of the children hadn't been so apparent the gathering could have been a social occasion.

Dr. Vallejo escorted me into his examining room and surgery. One metal cabinet housed every instrument he owned with the exception of a small electric sterilizer. The surgery table lacked even a thin pad and the surface shone coldly. Everything was immaculately clean. For that matter, Dr. Vallejo was attired in a long, white starched coat which reached the toes of his shoes.

We ambled into the wards. The bedclothes gleamed with the brightness all white fabric seemed to possess in Mistrató. Barely concealed by the gleaming counterpanes were scanty straw mattresses like the one which padded the bed in Richard's house. The simple unpainted wood frames supporting the straw were nothing more than low tables.

"I can help the patient get well, but as soon as he goes home he returns to the same behavior which created the illness." Dr. Vallejo's face tightened in anger. "After the patient is well, he seldom believes any of my warnings. The townspeople think I have magic. If my magic doesn't work, it was God's will the person should die, and who is to question God?"

The mountain air blew through the open windows of the wards bringing the scent of unknown flowers.

"But the worst thing is, I can see no remedy. The people are so poor I can't charge enough to purchase the instruments with which to do a better job. Part of the time I am even without hypodermic needles. The ones you send Richard he shares with me. In return he uses my sterilizer."

Some of the veterinary needles I'd sent had been the diameter of a match. I cringed and the doctor smiled.

"Not all the needles, just the smaller ones. So you see how desperate we are for equipment."

There was a discussion about asking medical people in the States for discarded instruments. I promised to see what could be done. We parted on the hope that somehow I would be able to locate the microscope he and Richard needed.

Richard was at the house when I returned. I told him about my tour of the hospital. His head bobbed in agreement as I talked. "We do need a microscope. I explain why an animal got sick but behind my back they look at each other and tap their temples with their forefingers. They tell each other, 'It's an idea of the gringo's—all those little animals you can't see.' "

He chopped off a piece of bread, slathered it with melting oleo, and took a bite. "I've got to make some calls this afternoon. Why don't you come with me and see for yourself?"

When he'd gulped down his substitute for lunch we left on his first call. After passing through a house, we entered a corral which contained two ponderously fat white hogs. Each was sporting a flannel necktie.

Richard's hands slid over their monstrous bodies, probing and checking. In a moment he straightened and walked toward the back porch where the wife was washing dishes. He held his hands upward, elbows bent, in the gesture see so often on medical television shows.

The woman stepped aside, handing him a bar of soap.

He made an effort to remove the dishpan from beneath the water tap but she shook her head. With a shrug he began washing his hands, the suds falling into her dishwater. A moment later she handed him her dishtowel.

As he vigorously dried his hands and forearms he frowned at me, a glower of significance. When we were back on the street he erupted.

"Now you see! The germs from the hogs have traveled to the family dishes, and so the contamination spreads! There's no use explaining. They don't believe me."

"Why were those rags tied around the hogs' necks?"

"Oh, the hogs have the mumps. There's no specific treatment for mumps in hogs. They usually get over the mumps whether you do anything for them or not. The local belief is that flannel soaked in lemon juice is the cure. So, just to keep on good terms, I go along with the treatment and tell the owner the medication is working fine."

"The hogs were certainly fat."

"Because they live on sugar cane. You can't build meat out of sugar. When they're butchered they'll be mostly lard."

While we talked we had arrived at the next address. In this corral were pens of rabbits, one of Richard's original projects when he began work in Mistrató. He'd written about his hope for rapid meat production from the rabbits. Enthusiasm had radiated from his letter. And then there was no further mention of the rabbits. Maybe the participants had gone ahead with the enterprise and Richard wasn't called in unless there was sickness.

One rabbit in the cage was dead, while the three others, although large and luxuriantly furred, were listless and panting. Richard removed the dead animal and examined it. A respectful silence accompanied the inspection. Then he turned back to the cage, his finger pointing.

Water dishes were spotted with feces. Food dishes contained spoiled vegetables with fresh rations thrown on top. The wire floor was littered with excreta, so clumped it would no longer fall through the mesh to the pile below, already drawing swarms of flies.

Angrily Richard threw out all the food and water and scrubbed the containers. He cleaned the cage, instructing that the debris be carted away to ferment in some other location. And as he worked, he talked in a voice cold with fury.

Two of the words he used were 'dirty' and 'responsibility.' The family listened in silence but when Richard's back was turned I saw the gesture he'd mentioned. The owner tapped his temple with his finger and glanced at his wife. She smiled and nodded. Unbidden, a memory popped into my head. The smiles were the same as those greeting my explanation of why one shouldn't squeeze the nipple of a nursing bottle and then give it back, unwashed, to the baby.

After the cage was clean and a lackadaisical effort was commenced to haul away the refuse, Richard turned to leave. "We have to go back to the house. I need antibiotics for the drinking water so the rest of the rabbits won't die." He tore out of the house and down the street so fast I had to trot to keep up with him.

"It's a great idea to call the gringo to bring medicine and save the animals," he ranted, "but when it's time to do a little work themselves they won't lift a finger. That's why I quit on the rabbit project. Most of the animals died from illnesses resulting from neglect. Sometimes I don't care if the whole damn town starves!"

We walked in silence for perhaps half a block.

"You never can tell," he went on, his eyes blank with concentration, "if I had a microscope and could show them the germs, they might believe me."

But the resistance to new ideas wasn't one hundred per cent. While Richard was measuring out the precious drug for the rabbit water, a tall, dark-visaged man in the white clothing of the mountaineer rapped at our door. Richard called for him to enter.

Sandaled feet stepped into the house while a hand swept off a hat, holding it by the chin strap which secures the huge sombrero when riding. Worriedly, the man began his tale.

Richard listened, continuing to measure and seal minute doses in ridiculously large bottles, bottles which once contained beer, soft drinks or the local licorice-fermented *aguardiente*. When the bottles were capped, he and the caller squatted to discuss the emergency.

The mountaineer told a lengthy tale and then answered Richard's questions. In a few minutes Richard took a prescription pad from his pocket and scribbled a formula, handing it to the caller. The man stared blankly at the paper.

Richard tried another tack. He pointed out the nearest drugstore and told the man to get the medicine and return.

A brown hand opened for Richard to take a fee. He glanced at the quantity of money in the open palm and then shook his head. With thanks the man turned away, heading for the pharmacy.

"Everyone tells me to charge. They say the money will buy drugs for the poorest farmers. They also say no one respects free advice. But I can't charge. That man has only enough for the medicine."

"Why is he coming back?"

"He can't read. He will have to memorize the directions for the medicine."

"What if he forgets on his way home?"

"He won't forget. The cow is his fortune."

A few minutes later the man returned with the medicine in his hand. Richard gave precise instructions, having the man repeat each phrase. When the caller could recite the whole combination of dosage and treatment, the two men shook hands and the mountaineer touched his forehead and chest in a blessing. He left in a cloud of dust kicked up by a horse startled at the urging of an impatient rider.

"Will he do everything you told him?"

"Yes, but for every man who follows instructions I have nine more that won't." He packed the pathetic array of bottles. "About the time I think my efforts are useless I get a good one like this man. I suppose that's what keeps me trying. You want to come with me?"

I shook my head. "I've seen enough."

He stopped on his way out the door. "It's just as bad for Dr. Vallejo. He doesn't try to explain about germs but he does go through a rigamarole about improper handling of spoiled food and body wastes making people sick. They condemn him with the remark, 'He got it all out of a book. He doesn't know anything about real life.'"

He stepped back inside the door and lowered his voice. "You want to hear about a debacle?"

I raised my eyebrows.

"The drugstores began to stock sanitary napkins because the doctor requested them. Pretty soon he started getting a whole lot of vaginal disorders. He couldn't figure it out. So he went down to the drugstore to see what brand they were carrying."

He paused and broke into a chuckle.

"You know what the trouble was? The drugstore had the cart before the horse. They'd bought napkins but no belts and the napkins were selling. The women were too embarrassed to ask how to use them so they were tearing them into pieces and trying to insert them. After he found that out he had his nurses explain to every woman who came to his office how the napkins should be used."

Shaking his head, he turned away and stepped outside.

"Thank God I don't have to work on people. When an animal dies I always wonder if I missed something I should have noticed, or if I neglected it. I don't think I could stand watching people die and wondering the same things."

As I closed the door behind him the suspicion crossed

my mind that a microscope might prove to be only a further frustration to Richard. Dr. Vallejo would be able to identify his bacteria but how convincing would the sight of those darting germs beneath the lens be to a person who couldn't read or write? The local gentry could stare through the instrument and still believe Richard had contrived a clever trick to prove his contention there were little animals one couldn't see.

However, if a microscope could be found, it would be sent. What Dr. Vallejo and Richard did with it after it arrived was their problem.

8
A Perilous Journey

Although Richard always rode the airline whose planes fell down oftener, I didn't suspect the extremes to which he carried this fatalistic point of view. His lack of prudence was strikingly shown by a trip he made far into the interior to organize a tribe of Indians and neighboring farmers.

The meeting was the result of many discussions with Luis Hacha, "The Ax." Hacha was Chief of the tribe and the accepted leader of neighboring small farmers. Every mention of a project involving Indians had prompted the same advice: "See The Ax."

The Indians were suspicious of all outsiders, and if Richard had been a surprise to Mistrató he was a miracle to the Indians. That a gringo should come to talk of improving their lot was an astonishment which had not occurred in the memory of any. Such a marvel should speak to no one of lesser importance than The Ax.

There was one small difficulty. The Ax was in jail, back in Mistrató.

"I'd seen the man," Richard said. "He wasn't much to look at with his long black hair and a face so ridged from old machete scars it looked like he'd been run over with a half-track. I guess you might say he had the reputation of an old western gunfighter. The more fights he won, the more men that challenged him. That's why he was always getting arrested. Anytime there's a fight, everyone goes to jail until the authorities place the blame."

Richard stopped gathering clothing and stuffing it into his saddlebags long enough to explain further. "Hacha doesn't stay inside the jail because the police know he isn't going to disappear. The arguments about fights always come out in his favor."

"How old a man is he?"

"About 45. He has four children but no sons. I'm supposed to meet with his group today but they don't have calendars so I don't know if there will be a meeting or not."

He flung his bulging saddlebags over his shoulder and started for the door. "Don't worry if I don't make it back tonight. It's getting ready to rain and this is the beginning of the rainy season so it may last all day. It's safe though." With this cryptic remark he left, his mounted figure urging the little mare into a run through the first spattering of raindrops freckling the dust layer in the street.

The heavens, which daily gave the jungle a cool drink,

turned dark and dripped and gushed by turns. At the supper hour Richard had not returned. Mario and Albero were absent, too. It was nearly midnight when a sopping Albero appeared. As soon as he changed into dry garments he came into our room.

"Richard's not back?"

"No." I reported the purpose of the trip.

"He's waited for this opportunity for a long time. Don't worry, *Mamacita*. Sometimes he's gone for a week, staying with different farmers at night. He's all right— the weather is warm."

This was the second mention of the weather in connection with a safe trip. I inquired what the relationship was.

"His horse won't fall."

"Fall?"

"Like the other time when it fell on Richard."

Richard's letters had reported no such event. Albero didn't know he was talking about something Richard had conveniently forgotten to tell me. Maternal sneakiness prompted me to be casual.

"He was lucky not to get hurt, wasn't he?"

Albero rubbed his wet head with one of our new towels.

"Not so lucky. He was black and blue and couldn't walk very well for a week. There was ice on the grass and the horse slipped over the edge. It rolled over him twice before he could free himself. Richard must have been unconscious a while because it was morning when he got home."

The room had taken on a chill. To be sure I wasn't mistaken in my translation I had Albero repeat his words.

"But he's been fortunate not to have anything worse happen, hasn't he?" I wangled.

Albero's eyes settled on my face. He didn't interpret my frozen smile as one of fear.

"Yes, the only other time we were really worried was when he started for the Peace Corps doctor and didn't make it." Albero frowned. "I knew he was sick that morning but he wouldn't listen. He took off for the mountains before I left for work. At noon I heard he'd hired a taxi-driver to take him to the doctor, but they didn't get there. That night the taxi-driver told everyone Richard had fallen unconscious on the street and he was in a hospital in a little town."

The room wasn't merely cold, it was freezing. What had happened to those wonderful safeguards I'd been told about, the helicopter that picked up a sick Volunteer, the stateside trained doctor always standing in readiness? Albero's story of a temperature rising to 105æ, the use of native medicines, and the excitement of the Peace Corps staff when they discovered Richard's predicament was a terrifying exposure.

"How long was he in the little hospital?"

"A week. Then he was ordered into Bogotá for a complete physical by the Peace Corps doctor." The only news filtering back to the States had been the unexpected physical examination in Bogotá, a summons which further reinforced my impression of constant care.

Albero turned away to retire, unaware he had sown

EIGHT

a whirlwind of disillusionment.

That night the wind howled louder and the rain drummed harder. I lay in bed imagining a muddy slip of Richard's horse plunging them into a fatal descent.

Next morning the sun was out in all its normal ferocious glory and by noon the mud had hardened. Women draped bedclothes on bushes, drying them from the night's leaks in the roofs.

Shortly after noon Richard returned. Mud caked the flanks and legs of his horse. His clothes were sodden, baking into stiff, muddy wrinkles. The hat on his head sagged like a flop-brimmed Panama. He looked exhausted. On his heels came Doje—who seemed equipped with radar—to take the mare for a bath and rubdown with oil.

When Doje led the horse away Richard got out of his soggy clothing and under the shower tap. After he donned fresh clothes he sat on the bench while I fixed a makeshift meal. "The rain slowed me down so much I didn't get to the meeting place until 9 o'clock last night," he said. "It was supposed to be an afternoon meeting."

"So you didn't get to organize after all?"

"Oh, yes. We had the meeting. But getting there was one of the hairiest trips I've ever made. It was dark before I arrived at the meeting place and I had to follow the trail by flashlight. The rain was coming down in torrents and the light barely showed the ground beneath the horse's feet. Finally I saw a flickering light from a window and knew I was on the right trail. When I got to the house, four men were waiting for me."

He scratched his ear thoughtfully.

"They got on their horses and we took off like bats out of hell. There were two horses in front of me and one behind but I couldn't see a damn thing. Rain was running down my glasses and the night was pitch black. We tore along a narrow jungle path with the wet branches switching my face. All I could hear was the wind and rain and horses feet clopping through the mud. It was wild!"

Red welts striped his face and arms where the branches had flayed him.

"We went down a steep hill, through a river, and climbed halfway back up the other side of the hill to a house. Several men came out and took care of our horses while we went inside."

An ecstatic smile lit up his face.

"There were forty people in that house waiting to hear me speak. I was so overcome with gratitude I nearly bawled. The Ax had persuaded those people to come. I hadn't expected more than five or six.

"First I had to change my clothes and then eat the chicken they'd fixed for me. It must have been ten o'clock by then. When I started talking the kids had gone to sleep, draped over their parents' laps because it was so crowded there wasn't room to lie on the floor. The whole place was steaming with clothes and the stench was so bad it was suffocating."

He stared out the door, opened to let the sun burn away the moldy odor the rain had incubated.

"That's the biggest organizational meeting I've ever had. The Ax is a dictator—benevolent, but still a dictator. You sure cut out a lot of red tape when there's a dictator.

The boy with the brains just decides what is best for everyone and tells them to do it."

He frowned at me. "Of course, the minute the Indians begin to think for themselves he'll have trouble."

"Does he know it?"

"Yeah. When he dies there will be no Chief and he wants the people to learn to govern themselves."

My thoughts reverted to the information Albero had let slip. "Why didn't you tell me about the time the horse fell with you?"

"Oh, that. It was a crazy accident. I was coming home at dusk when the rain turned into sleet. We were moving at a fast clip. The mare skidded and lost her footing and both of us went over the side of the mountain. We slammed into trees, crashed through bushes with the horse flailing her legs and me fighting to get free of the saddle. The last thing I remember is feeling my legs come loose and hearing her thrash on past me. When I came to my senses I was nearly frozen and covered with a layer of sleet, but the horse was all right and waiting for me farther down the mountain."

His description of lying unconscious in the sleet on a lonely mountain provided grist for motherly nightmares for the rest of his tour.

"Nobody came by that saw you?"

"I could have been dead a week before anyone happened to use that trail." He shrugged. "It wasn't my time."

I'd already heard more about his perils than was comfortable but a masochistic curiosity prodded me. "What about the time you didn't make it to the doctor?"

His eyes narrowed. "Who told you about that?"

"Somebody in town." Albero did live in town.

"That was plain stupidity on my part. I didn't feel well in the morning but there was something I wanted to finish before I went to the doctor. I was in the mountains before I realized my vision was blurring. When I got back to town and took my temperature it was 103° so I started for the doctor.

"But the doctor was five hours away and three hours later I passed out. Some people on the street carried me into a little local hospital."

"Why didn't you write home about this?"

"What could you have done?"

Ideas swam in my head of long distance calls, a precipitate trip to Colombia, hell-raising with the Peace Corps in Washington. What would I have done?

A slow grin was creasing Richard's face as he waited for my answer. When none came, he began to chuckle. "Are you planning on joining the service with me and telling me when to duck the bullets?"

With one teasing remark he'd snipped his final apron string. Thirty years of motherhood had ended. The ability to interpret a howl of anger, a wail of pain, a shriek of fear had become expendable. The later concerns of a first driver's license, youthful love affairs, drug temptations, and career guidance were also no longer my concern.

Someone has said the successful parent rears a child to fly freely away from the nest. Why wasn't I feeling proud instead of battling a slight nausea? Nothing had changed in the last ten minutes, except that I'd discovered what Richard had already known.

He didn't belabor the point but returned to discussing his meeting. I listened with half an ear. When he'd talked himself out and left on an errand, I worried. I couldn't go home and leave Richard in constant danger. Neither could I stay. I wouldn't be welcome even if I could arrange it!

Would it be possible, through some monumental maternal tantrum, to inveigle him into coming home with me? It wasn't likely. I was helpless to do anything for him or his safety. No answer was left to me but prayer.

I'd simply have to abide, or endure as they said it in Mistrató, waiting to see if his time came before he reached home again.

9

Where Is Your Woman?

The first question everyone asked when Richard moved into Mistrató was "Why did you come here?" The second was "Where is your woman?"

The vexations Richard had in trying to find a satisfying answer were now extended to me. They were asking me the same thing but phrasing it differently.

"Does Richard live at home or with someone else?" Doña Albertina inquired.

"At home, when he's not in school."

"Is he engaged?"

"Not unless he's engaged to someone in Colombia."

"Have you picked his wife in the United States?" Her eyes were riveted to my face.

I laughed. "The mother doesn't pick the wife where I live."

Doña didn't smile with me. Her manner was puzzled. "He seems healthy. He trots at his work."

To be healthy and single was a conundrum to Doña. And others were equally inquisitive. I was besieged with trick questions.

"Do you have a picture of Richard's fiancée?" was the way one person inquired.

"Will Richard marry as soon as he returns home?" had been another's method.

"Why didn't Richard's girl come with you?" had been one more attempt to get a different answer.

Each time I gave the same information, and knowing the speed of the grapevine, it was evident everyone knew what I was saying and nobody believed me. I was exasperated by their harping when I told Richard about it.

"Yeah, they didn't believe me either. No matter what I said they expected me to bring a girl, or get a local girl to move in with me. It's a town topic. I didn't know I was the subject of such absorbing speculation until I rented this house and invited Mario and Albero to share it."

"Did they ask about it?"

"Indirectly. They beat around the bush for a while and finally it hit me—they were asking if I was a homosexual!"

Richard had spent some time explaining that young men in the States often delay marriage, or even a serious commitment until the completion of their education is in sight.

"But what does a man do about his sex life?" Mario had asked.

"What do you do about it? Your dates are chaperoned."

"We go to the Zone," Albero said.

Then followed a tale of introduction to the prostitutes by an older male relative. Stories of parties given in honor of a boy's first visit were told. These celebrations took place in the Zone and all other male members of the initiate's family as well as his peers were invited. Richard found the open family sanction of the son's debut among the prostitutes as incomprehensible as Mario and Albero regarded the pretense of celibacy followed by monogamy in stateside behavior.

However, the boys achieved an understanding and agreed to share the house. Mario and Albero suggested a remedy to end the rumors about Richard. "You must let us arrange dates for the nights you are in town."

"O.K. I'll plan my work to be home more often in the evenings."

A few days later he went on his first date with a town girl. It had the effect of a formal announcement: "The gringo is looking for a wife." In a week's time he was swamped with invitations.

Every man in town with a daughter between the ages of thirteen and twenty invited him for a meal. The one-sided courtship was the result of a conviction that the gringo had secret wealth. His sudden popularity threatened the growing acceptance of his work by the town.

To refuse an invitation meant the daughter had been rejected without even the courtesy of a first call. To accept every bid would result in impossible social complications. It was a dilemma.

Carefully wording his request, he pleaded with his housemates to get him out of the predicament. They began sidetracking pursuing fathers but no one believed their explanations of the time-consuming requirements of Richard's work.

"The gringo is very particular," the townspeople told each other.

"That stopped the dinner invitations," Richard continued, "but the talk goes on. The reason they are so interested in my private life is that they think food, drink, and sex are daily necessities."

"Daily?"

Richard nodded. "A man expects to make love every time he gets into bed. If there are thirty days in the month, then he expects to have intercourse thirty times, plus any little side trips to the Zone."

"That's quite a schedule! What do the women think about it?"

"They expect it. If a man doesn't make love to his wife every day she goes into a decline worrying about her femininity." His brows knit as he grinned wryly. "That could get to be a real drag, trying to be romantic seven days a week no matter how either one of you felt."

I thought his opinion was understated!

"Are they this curious about the priest? They know every detail of his life and see there are no women in it."

"Oh, that's different. When the Father took his vows God removed all his fleshly desires."

"That's a handy conclusion."

"Yeah, the priest laughs about it. I go around with

the Padre and some of the people think I'm very religious. A few think that God removed my fleshly desires too because of my work, but they're in the minority."

Richard laughed and then shook his head. "Everything here connected with male and female is very complicated. 'Everyone knows' that the attraction between man and woman is uncontrollable. At the first opportunity they leap into bed together. It is inevitable!"

"And it's nobody's fault."

"Of course not. It is to be expected. The only people who disagree are the Padre, the doctor, the mayor, and Luis Hacha. The Ax has little formal education but he's brilliant. He started an argument in his group over this point that will go on for months. The club's first project was a two-room school. One room was for the boys and the other for the girls. I wanted to have two grades, all the children in the first grade in one room and all second-graders in the other." He grinned. "That suggestion blew their minds. They said any sensible person knew what would happen. Within a month every girl in school would be raped."

The sun slanting through our door wasn't any brighter than Richard's face. "You know what? That old Indian chief stood up and told them why the old ways had to go. He said progress meant new ideas and that man is smarter than animals and therefore has control over his urges. He said anyone who thought otherwise was ignorant. He accused every man in the room of sexual irresponsibility."

"Did anyone leave?"

"No, the whole group listened. Then the Chief start-

ed talking about women being human and not beasts to
be used for reproduction or physical pleasure and some
of the women put their hands over their faces in embarrassment. But they peeked through their fingers and
listened to every word."

It seemed incongruous: a women's liberation front
promoted by an Indian chief.

"Then he told them about marriage in the States.
He'd asked me dozens of questions before I got the club
organized. He finished by pointing out the kind of work
load I carried and yet had no woman living in my house."
Richard snorted. "That made me an oddity."

"What did they decide about the school?"

"It isn't decided yet. But they're building and they're
arguing. I'm betting on the old man. He'll talk them into
two grades before the school is completed."

"How far along is the building?"

"About half way. When I go out to see how they're
doing, some woman is sure to get me aside and ask if it's
true that a man has only one wife in the United States and
no little *casitas*."

"Little casitas?"

"Other smaller houses where the mistresses live. As
soon as you get two dimes to rub together you set up a
little casita, one woman to a house, and the more women
you have on tap the more important you are."

"Do the wives know about these other women?"

"Usually they do. But then this is the same kind of
life their mothers lived. They don't seem to care much
what the husband does as long as he supports the family.

If he gets too out-of-line the wives have their own ways of in-fighting. There's no divorce, you know, so the women have a guarantee that the husband has to put up with whatever meanness the wife thinks up."

It occurred to me I hadn't seen any flirting with Richard in Mistrató. There was a gap somewhere between the popularity he reported and his present indifferent treatment.

"I assume something happened that ended your eligibility."

"Oh, yes." His eyebrows raised and he laughed. "It not only eliminated me as a desirable son-in-law, it earned me the rating of *macho* at the same time!"

"What happened?"

"A couple of girl Volunteers came through. All Volunteers have keys to each other's houses and they use the house whether anyone is home or not. Mario and Albero had gone on vacation and I was out in the mountains when the girls arrived. Coming through town on my return everyone looked at me. I couldn't figure it out. But when I walked in the door the mystery was explained. There was girls' lingerie on my clothesline."

"The girls came back that evening and we tacked a poncho over the arch. I slept in Mario's room, but nobody in town believed it. The girls left the next day before my housemates got home."

"Did you tell Mario and Albero about it?"

"They'd heard the story before they reached the house. They could hardly wait to tell me what people were saying.

"'People are saying, the gringo isn't interested in one woman at a time. He needs two.'"

Richard jumped to his feet and with bent elbows clamped to his waistline, he clenched his fists in front of him and jerked his body in a bump.

"That means *macho*. They thought the girls and I were indulging in some exotic kind of sex. Even Mario and Albero don't believe my version of the incident."

"Nobody's trying to promote a wedding now," he chortled. "They don't want their daughters taught the kind of sex the gringo needs. Albero says everytime I come to town some man is sure to say 'Lock up your daughters. Here comes the *macho* gringo!'"

10
The Shopping Tour

Sunday was market day in Mistrató. Before the sun
pierced the lingering night mist in the mountains, farmers
trudged into town, their merchandise on their bent backs
or loaded astraddle an animal. Voices called to each other
as friends who had been separated for a week met again.
Early churchgoers stayed in town after the services. It
was the only day in the week that so many people were
in town at once.

I had my own reasons for anticipating the day. With
the produce and meat at the market I could improve our
depressingly dull meals and possibly experiment with
some native dishes. Richard would accompany me to do
the bargaining that my own Spanish would not cover.

However, when I awakened, a note hung on his desk telling of an early call for a sick cow. I dressed and waited until nearly noon when Albero appeared.

"You're not going shopping?"

I explained my plight.

"But, of course, I will take you myself and see that you do not pay too much for the food."

Gratefully I accepted his offer and we set off.

As we entered the town square my first impression was that we'd inadvertently stumbled into a war. At least fifteen uniformed men, dressed in the shade of green we see on the U.S. Army, stood about the block. Under each left arm an automatic machine gun dangled carelessly from a cross-shoulder strap.

"Who are those men?"

"The police. The shift is changing. There are 32 of them. Every three months they change locations and on the day they move to another area they get their new assignments in Mistrató."

"Are all of them armed the same way?"

"Yes."

"Are they guarding the plaza today?"

Albero smiled. "No, *Mamacita*, they are visiting friends just as everyone is. It is a rule they must wear their uniforms at all times."

Reassured, I turned my attention to the produce. A group of sacks were folded back to expose undersized, red pitted potatoes. Great piles of yucca, shaped like sweet potatoes but trailing feathery roots, occupied another square of ground. Several huge stalks of plátano were exhibited nearby. Dark green, smooth-skinned avocados crowded each other in a wicker basket. We stopped to purchase a few.

As I selected several ripe ones, Albero interrupted.

"No, no. Pick one ripe fruit and then choose each one a little firmer than the last. Because they are at different stages of maturity they will be ready to eat, one at a time as the days pass."

Why hadn't I thought of that? It was the only sensible method if one had no refrigeration.

When it was time to pay, Albero was very firm. I caught part of his words. He disputed the rumor that the gringa was rich and could afford to pay any price asked. Finally the men agreed but when we walked away Albero was irritated.

"We paid too much. He will sell to others for less." He regarded it as a personal defeat.

We stopped at a huge tree where two hogs and a cow were tethered. Their owners expounded the virtues of the animals but Albero shook his head. A man approached us with a cat in his arms. The animal was thin to the point of emaciation. The men ignored the cat's condition and discussed the merits of owning such an animal. Albero waxed enthusiastic but I decided to let Richard choose any cat we might acquire.

Our interest in the animals had been noticed. A woman with a dog secured by a string stopped us. She and Albero engaged in a lengthy conversation while the dog and I eyed each other. The woman had all the assurance of someone in possession of a gold ingot. When the conversation ended Albero explained.

"She has a paca dog for sale. It is very expensive, $300 American."

I glanced back at the skinny dog to see what prompted the excessive asking price. "She must be crazy."

"No, she will get that amount from someone."

"In Mistrató?"

"Not from anyone who lives here. There are men here from other areas."

Scattered about were a few men dressed in better clothes than the crowd.

"They come to these small markets looking for paca dogs. This dog is one of the most prized possessions a man can have."

"Are they show dogs?"

Albero shook his head. "They are hunters. We have an animal called a paca. It is a delicacy and much prized for rich men's tables. The meat is similar to chicken but much better. A paca dog can track down this animal and catch it. He's trained for the purpose."

"What does a paca look like?"

"A small kangaroo." Albero laughed. "Richard says it's nothing but a big rat. There are many of them in the rain forest. A man with a good dog could provide meat for a banquet out of a small area."

We were passing tables displaying breads and cookies while we talked. As all the other local breadstuffs, they were dyed improbable shades of blue, yellow, green, or Pepto-Bismol pink. The sweet rolls offered were thick circles of bread sprinkled with *panela*. Cookies baked from the coarsely ground corn were spotted with lunching insects.

Opposite the church stood a row of meat stands with overhead awnings. Each booth was staffed by two or three men. Instead of the deep red beef or pink pork cuts our groceries display, these cuts defied identification. And as we moved closer, there were added attractions!

Balanced in a neat pyramid on the ground were four feet and shinbones of a cow. What Mistratóans did with these it was impossible to imagine. Two stands further on a hog skull, still equipped with staring blue eyes almost jumping out of the sockets from which the lids had been trimmed, goggled at us. This was the meat selection from which I expected to vary our meals!

No explanations were necessary. Albero read my blank expression easily. We drifted over to a crowd of people surrounding a table over which towered the tallest man I'd seen in town. He could look over the heads of the people gathered to purchase his wares.

He was not only the tallest man, he had a neat beard and was well-dressed. Albero said he was the witch-doctor. As people made purchases and left, we edged forward through the crowd. On the table were dozens of items whose use was unfathomable. Albero pointed to several, telling me what they were and why they were in demand.

"That's ground-up snails, for hexes. There is bear hair, bear claws, and ground up bear claws—for witch-craft, too. The bottles contain snake oil, to rub on yourself or to drink to cure sickness. The assortment of berries and herbs are medicines for stomach ailments or dysentery. The little jar contains pickled octopus, for putting a curse on an enemy."

The bearded man exchanged a bottle of medicine for money. The label was printed in English and was a well-known patent remedy also selling in the States.

"The soap is for skin ailments," Albero continued. Pink, brown, and black bars were stacked on one corner.

"The colors tell what ailment they cure. And that other thing is coca (cocaine in crude form). It's used for pain."

The witch-doctor was doing a brisk business. At the outer edge of the group I spied Dr. Vallejo watching the proceedings. As he caught my eye he shook his head as if to say, "This is what I'm up against."

For a while we watched the eager purchasing and then sauntered over to the only part of the market we'd missed. Women sitting on the ground held up links of sausage for our approval. Their voices extolled the wares.

The meat looked appetizing; coming from the steaming iron pots of hot water it might be sterile. I stepped nearer to inspect the open end of the sausage.

It was darker than most unsmoked sausage but it was tempting. I turned to ask Albero to purchase some for us and met a tense expression.

Instead of questioning him I merely asked, "We don't buy this?"

Relieved, he shook his head.

"Are you through shopping?" He dropped his gaze to the few avocados I held.

"Yes."

Albero shrugged. There was no accounting for what the gringa did.

"I must attend to my business then."

As he left I thanked him for his trouble and headed toward home. It was clear the market was no solution to our uninspired menus. The matter wasn't as important as it seemed several days ago. The sausage had looked better than anything else at market and yet Albero hadn't wanted me to buy it. I must remember to ask Richard the reason.

Richard didn't come home until evening. He had arrived at the farm with the sick cow to find several other farmers waiting to take him to tend their own sick animals. Before the trip was over he'd made six calls on different farms miles apart.

After a tiresome supper of tuna fish with chopped onion which we laughingly described as salad, we discussed the day. I told of the things I'd seen at market.

"Albero didn't want me to buy the sausage," I reported as I ended my tale.

Richard looked at me over his glasses.

"He knew I wouldn't eat it."

"Why? It came out of boiling water."

"Don't let that steam fool you. If you stuck a thermometer in one of those links the heat wouldn't even be up to body temperature. The meat is in the hot water just long enough to warm it. It's actually raw."

"But it looked as dark as Italian smoked sausage. Maybe it's cured or treated before they bring it to market."

"No it isn't. The vendor probably mixed it up yesterday. The brown color is dye. You've probably noticed they dye many of the foods here. That sausage is the worst of all. If that concoction doesn't kill you, nothing will! Do you know what they put into it? Gristle, fat, bananas, onions, salt, ground up cow feet, and any cockroaches that happen to fall in. I've seen it mixed."

"So that's what they do with feet and shinbones!"

"Yep."

"How do they use the hogs heads?"

"Boil them." He shuddered. "The eyes are a delicacy. The whole head is cooked in sort of a stew but before it is served the eyes are fished out and given to the father or any guest eating with them."

I tried to put the imagined sensation out of my head.

"That's why I've refused all dinner invitations except the one from Doña Albertina. She never cooks hogs heads, so I knew you wouldn't run into trouble. I was afraid if we ate with someone and they served you hog eyes you might faint. It could be very embarrassing for me."

How thoughtful! What filial devotion! His only concern was not for my delicate sensibilities but that I might swoon and disgrace him. But, of course, he was quite accurate in guessing my reaction to such a token of esteem. It was an honor I'd been glad to miss.

During the evening, after the disappointment of market, I grappled with new schemes for obtaining food.

"Where is the nearest place one can find a selection of groceries?"

TEN

"Anserma." He watched me while I calculated. Three hours out and three back by taxi over a dangerous road.

"You can go tomorrow if you want." His eyes were curious. "Are you that hungry? I haven't been hungry in months."

Now that he asked, I realized I wasn't hungry at all. The routine of preparing meals was an unsuitable habit in these surroundings. The importance of market day faded into the background. Even though survival depended on a very limited number of staples, we weren't without food.

It wasn't required that one enjoy what he ate. The trick was to consume enough to keep the stomach comfortably full and swallow enough vitamins to offset the deficiencies. I'd noticed immediately that Richard paid little attention to what he ate. Now I understood how he'd arrived at that indifference. It was only a matter of adjusting your attitude to fit the possibilities.

11
"It Fell"

A singular theory permeated Mistrató. The people endowed all objects with a will of their own. Any accident was due to the obstinacy of a conflicting will or was commanded by God. Albero made the point one day when I dropped an egg and was disgusted with my own clumsiness.

"*Se cayó,*" he said soothingly. "It fell."

To his mind the accident had no connection with me. It was simply a sign the egg had chosen to thwart my purpose.

"I should have been more careful," I persisted.

"No, no," he patted my shoulder. "The egg didn't want to go into the skillet."

It was a curious evasion of responsibility and I mentioned it later to Richard.

"That's the hardest thing I have to combat. All the time people tell me 'God will take care of us, or if He doesn't, the government will.' They don't think they have any control over their lives." He jumped up and strode around the room.

"I keep preaching, 'Help is at hand, right at the end of your own two arms. Begin by helping yourselves.' And you know what they say? They whisper to each other about how the gringo thinks he can give orders to life. It's maddening."

"Is that the trouble with getting a bridge?"

He nodded.

On a jaunt Richard had shown me a gorge, dropping several hundred feet to the river. A narrow path writhed down across the river and snaked perilously up again. The place shouted for a bridge.

"When I talk about building a bridge, just a rope suspension unit, they tell me 'The mountain didn't want to make a bridge.' "

I remembered the tiny figures traversing the rugged trail.

"How many people use that path?"

"Nearly a hundred a day. You can't even ride a horse up or down that grade. They know a bridge would make the path much easier but I'm promoting a daring philosophy, this tampering with God's plans."

He stopped pacing and flopped on the bench. "But then I didn't think I'd get the road, and it's being built with no tools but hammers and shovels."

The road was a thin, rough lane laboriously being built from boulders hand-cracked into gravel. Months of work had already gone into it and only a few hundred yards were completed. It was a lifetime task, but it was a monument. Mayor García had mentioned it earlier.

"Did you see the road? It is a landmark. First we paved the plaza, and now we build a road," the mayor declaimed. "Mistrató will never be the same."

At the touting of his accomplishments, Richard took a sudden interest in a nearby bush. "It will take time," was his comment.

"That is what I usually tell you," the mayor said. "I am the one who holds back when you want so many new ordinances." His eyes turned to me.

"It is a problem. Most of the people are uneducated. When we make new ordinances, sometimes they do not understand and violence results. If I change too many things at once, some night I will be killed, and then who will help Richard?" The statement was delivered in banner headlines.

It must be an exaggeration. But Richard was agreeing!

"That's right. They tell him 'We got along fine before the gringo came. Why do you listen to him?' They think when Mayor García changes something because of me it is evidence that his mind isn't what it ought to be."

"We move only an inch at a time against decades of superstition," the mayor added, sounding as if he'd lifted the remark from some previous orator.

And nowhere were the traditional beliefs more apparent than in the attitudes toward death. A sign on a door saying 'Funeraria' had piqued my interest. I made a special trip one day to call on the owner. At my knock the frail, bright-eyed man invited me inside, sweeping his arm in a circle, bidding me make myself at home. The room was his showcase.

A gleaming buffed and polished dark wood casket sat in the center of the room. The interior was lined with gathered soft, white fabric but lacked the customary padding beneath. It was closed by a lid of narrowing terraces, rising to a long hinged panel perhaps eight inches wide. Underneath the slim door was a glass window.

"For the services," he explained as he demonstrated. "We close the casket when we prepare the body and then open this hinged slot for friends to have a last look."

"We have something similar in the States, but the glass is as wide as the casket and covers the whole opening. When the lid is lowered over the glass the casket is sealed airtight, to preserve the body."

"Oh, no, not to preserve the body." The wiry man swiftly crossed himself. "Ashes to ashes and dust to dust. The glass is to see but not to touch. The sheet might become disarranged. I drape it very carefully."

"Sheet?" My translation must be at fault.

"Yes, the cover for the body."

I had understood him correctly. "No clothes?"

"No. The living need the clothes. The dead do not. We bury only in a sheet." He glanced at the tiny, white diamond-shaped caskets hanging on every wall. "Did you notice these?"

"Oh, ah—remarkable!" Was I expected to admire the workmanship or bewail the number needed?

He seemed to wait for more minute appraisal so I stepped forward for a closer look. Each white lid had a gold foil cross in the center. The lids extended like eaves over the small oblong boxes. I glanced back at the mortician to ask a question but his happy smile drove it out of my head.

"We bury many babies," he beamed. "Many little ones stay only for a visit and fly on to heaven. Little angels, all of them, and so soon!"

His expression reflected delight at such blessed circumstances but he tore himself away from the inspiring contemplation to tell me more about his establishment. He was proud of his business and told me in detail his favored methods of embalming, even pulling up his shirt to show at what point he injected the preservative.

"It keeps the body in beautiful condition. If the family permits me to use it, we don't have to bury the body until the next day."

This statement didn't bear speculation. I thanked him and left, puzzling over his pleasure at the number of baby funerals. But his attitude was no more bewildering than the parental placidity in the face of illness. It was a peculiarity in the abstract but a devastating experience to watch. The sickness of the baby next door was an illustration.

For several days the baby cried more frequently. It wasn't the indignant howl of an American child. This sound was more nearly that of a mewing kitten. One afternoon the cry was noticeably weaker. I peeked over the fence to see the mother sitting on the step, her body rocking back and forth, making a half-hearted attempt to soothe the baby in her arms.

But her face above was untouched by anxiety, undisturbed by the child's misery. When Richard came in for supper I told him of the unconcerned expression and the baby's feeble cries.

He sat down at his desk and stuffed food in his mouth.

"It's dying." His jaws never lost a stroke. He ate several more mouthfuls before he noticed my stillness.

"I see it all the time." The indifference in his voice revolted me.

"Parasites? Or malnutrition?"

"One, or both, and curable." I'd heard more excitement in his voice over a sick chicken.

"What's the matter with you? Don't you care? You've got all that medicine in your locker. You could offer that family some help!"

He slowly masticated the mouthful and swallowed before he answered. His eyes were black with intensity.

"There's a doctor in this town and they won't take the baby to him. What makes you think they'd let a quack veterinarian prescribe? If the baby dies, it was because God called it and they'd tell me very quickly the matter was none of my business."

He took another bite, chewing automatically.

"My job here is to improve food and sanitation. If I succeed, maybe the next generation of babies won't die. But I can't fix everything. I have to concentrate on a few ideas and hammer over and over on those points. If they understand the benefits, then they'll stay with the new ways after I've left. I'm trying to be part of the solution instead of getting spread so thin I only become a new part of the problem."

He turned back to his meal. As far as he was concerned the subject was closed. A muted whimper drifted through the open door, a sound to twist any mother's heart.

"Aren't you going to eat?" His face was impassive.

"I'm not very hungry." My appetite had fled.

Without turning his head, Richard slanted a look in my direction, a resigned smile curling his lips.

"Are you going to be part of the problem?"

It wasn't my intention. I filled my mouth with rice and chewed resolutely but my fork wavered through unshed tears. Richard ignored me.

Later that evening, when we settled down with my reading and his charts, he took pity on me. He knew I was hearing every frail plaint from next door.

"When I came to Mistrató I was overwhelmed with all the things that needed doing. Everywhere I looked there was a problem, an urgent one. For the first few months I ran myself ragged trying to do everything. I bled and I suffered. Eighteen-hour days weren't enough. I was behind on my work when I got up in the morning. Then I sized up the situation and saw I wasn't accomplishing what I came to do because there were too many distractions. I had to put on blinders to everything but my objective. You must do the same. Stuff your ears with cotton because you can't ease that baby's pain by hurting with it."

Somebody had said these things to him. He'd delivered the words in a lecture tone.

But his words had a mocking ring the following morning when the couple next door carried a tiny, blanket-wrapped figure in the direction of the Funeraria. Their faces above the bundle they carried were serene and acquiescent.

Bitter gringo judgements surged through my head. The baby's death was so wildly unnecessary and so nobly accepted at the same time. Ignorance and neglect had been made into a virtue. As the couple carrying the tiny corpse turned the corner I burst into helpless tears.

How valiant I'd thought the lyrics "Whatever will be, will be" when they lilted from the lips of Doris Day. But watching only one family following that precept engulfed me in futile rage.

Richard and the city fathers were fighting for comprehension from a population whose minds were so damaged by malnutrition and illness that their capacity to learn was limited. And another generation of brain-starved children was arriving. Richard hoped to save the next generation. It was already too late for nearly every adult in town!

As my tears dried, I realized the peasants' attitude of patient resignation was the only one which would enable them to stumble through the unpredictability of their daily lives. To understand their doom would be unbearable.

Maybe it was a blessing they didn't expect, to be in charge of their lives. They perceived themselves to be only spectators of the unfolding panorama of fate.

12

Improvise! Improvise!

"This town needs a girl Volunteer. I keep asking for one but when I explain about the living conditions here no girl will come."

Richard was writing his monthly reports for the Peace Corps.

"What would she do?"

"Same things I do, except with women. For example, she could start a home demonstration group. She could show the women how to make better use of what they have. Teach them to cook better meals too."

Had I heard that song before? He probably thought a girl could do all the wonders with Doña Albertina's cooking I wasn't equal to accomplishing.

"But there's so little available."

"Use what there is. The first week I was here I put up a fence post in the plaza. From the top of the pole I angled a rope to the ground and tied dozens of the vegetable fiber sponges around the rope. Then I saturated the sponges with animal dip solution. Beside the post I erected a sign telling the farmers how they could get rid of insects that plague animals by building the same thing. The animals would rub up against the sponges and the dip would kill the pests. There was a crowd around that pole all the time. A girl could set up a stove and show how to cook rice five different ways, for a starter."

Rice recipes clicked through my head. Spanish rice— no ground meat. Curried rice, no spices. Chicken and rice, no chicken. Rice and sausage, rice and ham, rice chowder, each had a problem because there was no meat or meat broth available.

"What else could you do with rice but boil it?"

"How about rice pudding?"

"That would take milk, eggs, and sugar, plus an oven. I guess *panela* could be ground up for the sugar."

"If you could find something to grate it on. Or you could put it between two layers of cloth and hammer it with a rock until it was fine enough."

That ought to be about as entertaining as peeling those potatoes with the table knife. But it could be done.

"Now about an oven . . ." he was frowning. "Why don't you go talk to Mr. Rosales, the baker. He has a big oven and he got it somewhere. Find out about it and while you're there take a good look at how it's built. Maybe we could copy it in a smaller size."

He turned back to his reports and the idea fermented. That afternoon I hunted out the bakery.

It was located in the corral behind a house. I had arrived too late to see any of the mixing of the dough. Maybe it was just as well.

Long wooden tables were lined beneath thickly foliaged trees. Loaves were heaped on the tables and another batch was coming out of the oven. The oven was a cylindrical structure of bricks and mortar, possibly eight feet tall. The assistant reached inside with a huge wooden spatula and lifted out a large black, metal cookie sheet containing several more of the loaves which looked as if they'd fallen during baking.

The young man filled a wicker basket with the bread as Mr. Rosales told me about the bakery business. He was delighted to have such an interested listener. The assistant swung the basket with its jumble of loaves to his shoulder and left, apparently on his way to make store deliveries.

Mr. Rosales and I talked while droppings from the multitude of birds attracted by the odor splashed on the uncovered loaves. Absentmindedly, the baker wiped away the traces as best he could with a dirty cloth hanging from his belt.

I pretended not to notice and made a mental note to trim the crust from our bread from now on.

"Do you bake cakes or pies?"

"Cakes I have seen. Pies? What are pies?"

With the benefit of sign language I explained a fruit pie. My listener paid close attention but it was the amused interest of discovering a queer custom.

"No, I have never seen this thing. We do not like fruit inside of bread in Mistrató."

We skipped to the subject of the oven. It had been constructed by local bricklayers and had been very expensive. I told of the stateside custom of each home being equipped with an oven. As I talked, suspicion spread over the baker's face.

"I do not think the women will want to go back to doing their own baking. They are used to the ease of buying their bread from me."

"The home ovens are not usually for bread. They are used to bake other things, sweets and puddings for their meals."

Mr. Rosales laughed. "Who would want to take all that trouble. Our women are spoiled by modern conveniences. They would not consider doing the extra work."

"You are probably right." I didn't think he was but had no wish to further antagonize him.

I'd already aroused his animosity. He saw my questions as leading to a diminished demand for his product. I hastened to placate him. The last thing I wanted to do was stir up hostility. With several complimentary remarks about the large production accomplished by two people and the appetizing smell which surrounded his bakery, I reassured him. His face resumed its former placidity. We parted as friends.

But as I walked away my mind was busy. Without his assistance I could probably manage a tin reflector oven which would fit on the sink-stove arrangement most kitchens in Mistrató had. The hardware store would have the things I needed to make it.

The merchandise in the windows of the hardware store was misleading. As I entered the dark, dusty interior I found nearly everything the store stocked was in the windows. A few kerosene lamps, extra chimneys, candles, and a few pairs of rubber boots were scattered among the empty shelves. I asked for tin and tin snips.

There was no tin in town and the proprietor had never heard of tin snips. While I was peering about the store I spied a roll of electric wiring, good quality, rubber-coated and free of dust. This must be the roll from which the priest purchased his wiring for his electric plant. There was plenty on the spool to make a long extension cord for hooking up a hot-plate on the plaza. Could rice pudding be cooked on top of a stove? It was worth a try.

And why couldn't one try the same thing with beans? Would it be possible to make baked beans in a pan? I'd find out. But how to start? First I must make a list and go to Anserma for some utensils. I headed home, with a wealth of ideas and buoyed up by the germ of inspiration.

When Richard saw my list he studied it silently.

"Yeah, you could do this, but if you have to go to Anserma for these things, where are the women going to get similar utensils?"

"But most of those things they have already, don't they?"

He shook his head, and pointed to the first item on the list.

"Eggbeater. Can you make this recipe with that native eggbeater on the wall?"

The dowel rod gadget and I had already had a fracas. Besides clogging with eggs, it spattered droplets as profusely as a lawn sprinkler. In addition, the serrated rings made it nearly impossible to clean. One using had been enough.

"You're beginning to get the idea, but you have to use what is here, not import things they can't buy in town."

"But the stores would stock these things if there were a demand, wouldn't they?"

"I doubt it. Remember the store owners have very little money and they can't afford to gamble. What if it turned out to be a fad, this new kind of cooking, and the women lost interest? Then the proprietor would be stuck with the merchandise."

His comment took the wind out of my sails. He knew he'd deflated me.

"It's a good idea but not practical enough. Keep thinking about it. You'll come up with something."

I tried to concentrate on improvisations but my mind creaked forward slowly. During each shopping trip I eyed the shelves, looking for items which could be put to broader use. Spying some flax seed in the drug store stirred an idea. I could invite some women to the house and show them how to make waving lotion for their hair with flax seed. A minute later I discarded the notion. Curly hair would be a rose for the spirit but an idiotic concern for women so malnourished they barely had enough energy to plough through each day. On the heels of that decision another idea hatched.

I would cut a pattern for a sanitary belt and show them how to make a comfortable one. In spite of the nurse's explanations, the change to outside application of the napkins hadn't been entirely a success. A network of strings was being used which must have been a constant annoyance. I could get a group together and show them how to make the belt in the privacy of a home.

That evening I outlined my ideas to Richard. He smiled.

"Now you've got it. Ask someone who has a sewing machine to have the meeting in her home. Help them cut the patterns and make one yourself while they watch. Then you can move on to the cooking. Use their utensils and go through the recipe step by step."

He elaborated on the theme, mentioning the fact that there were no cookbooks in Mistrató as so few could read.

"But if you go through the whole thing in front of them they'll remember every step. One thing you'll have to watch. Don't go too fast. Show them only one new thing at each meeting."

I was basking in the knowledge my brain had finally engaged when he jumped up from his desk and consulted the calendar. When he turned to face me his expression was rueful.

"You're not going to have time to get it rolling."

"Why not? I still have five days."

"But things take time here. When you suggest the idea you'll have to walk all over town and personally invite each woman. Every woman will accept but at the first meeting only three or four will come. You'll have to give four or five demonstrations before they decide they're missing something. That process will take most of a month."

He shook his head. "No, you just don't have enough time left." His expression was puzzled. "Why didn't you think of this sooner?"

It was a good question, but I wished he hadn't asked me. I didn't have a good answer.

13

The Chance of a Lifetime

The red light district in Mistrató was called the Zone. It operated as a country club, with certain alluring fringe benefits. Richard pointed it out to me on a town tour but it was a matter of indifferent interest at the time. I didn't expect to meet any of the residents. Apparently the Madam had other ideas.

On the way to town one morning, a short, satiny-skinned woman with waist-length hair dropped into step with me. The red sweater draped around her shoulders set off the brilliance of thick-lashed dark eyes.

Her conversation skipped the usual courtesies—a rare omission.

"Are you the mother of Ricardo?"

"Yes." I introduced myself, giving my full name.

She didn't offer hers. "Do you have other children?"

"A daughter."

"Why didn't she come with you?"

"The trip is very expensive."

"But that is of no importance. You are rich."

I repeated the story of my house without a maid.

"But if you aren't rich, why did Ricardo come here?"

"He wants to help people."

"Ah!" Her eyebrows raised. "He is very religious." She saw him as a missionary, an appellation Richard abhorred.

"Goodbye, *Señora*." Abruptly the walker broke away as we entered the plaza. Swinging the only bright-colored sweater I'd seen in town, she headed in another direction. I forgot her immediately.

Over supper that evening Richard asked, "Did you walk to town today with a woman in a red sweater?"

"Maybe. Yes, I think I did."

"That was the Madam."

"Of the Zone?"

He nodded. "I guess she wanted to meet you since everyone else has."

I recalled the woman's rather conservative appearance. She hadn't been draped with jewelry as the girls walking the streets in Pereira had been. She looked like any housewife in town and the women leaning out over their half-doors had greeted her as we passed.

"How did she get into that business?"

"Same way as most of them. Her folks were coffee growers. When she was about twelve there was a bad year for coffee and her folks gave her to a Madam. Her wages fed the family. When the family was in better circumstances she stayed on in the house and saved her money. She saw the possibilities and wanted a house of her own."

He sounded as matter of fact as if the woman had embarked on any other business venture.

"Is there a lot of VD because of her house?"

"No. She's licensed and the girls are inspected every week."

Unexpectedly he laughed. "There's some funny sidelights to her business. Some of the women are religious. When they take a customer to bed they assume the missionary position."

"What do you mean?"

"Flat on the back with arms outstretched to each side of the bed and eyes focused on a religious picture on the ceiling. The girl mumbles prayers while she carries out her duties."

"Doesn't the customer resent it?"

"Nope. Some men always choose the religious girls. He is grateful because she is getting them both forgiven while he's free to indulge. He'll claim he's cursed with a tremendous sex drive which can't be accommodated at home. It's a form of bragging."

"It doesn't sound like much to brag about."

"It isn't, but when your family is on the verge of starvation, half of your children are in the cemetery, and the ones still living are only waiting until they're old enough to leave, you don't have anything to crow about.

So the man brags to the prostitutes."

"What happens to the girls when they get old?"

Richard chortled. "Well, they don't brand an A on their foreheads and throw them out, if that's what you're asking! They've saved their money, or invested it, just like any other single woman in business."

People didn't talk so freely about such subjects during my tender years. What I knew about the oldest profession you could put in your eye.

"And then, of course, some of them marry out of the Zone." His eyes squinted, watching my expression. "You don't get it, do you? It's no disgrace to enter the Zone to feed your family. Any woman could be in the Zone except for luck."

He reached for another cup of the inky brew we called coffee before he continued.

"The Madam is mad at me."

"Why?" I was almost afraid to ask.

"The town was talking about wanting to pave the plaza when I got here. So I organized everyone and got the effort started. Everyone was asked to donate, time or money. I talked the Madam into giving the proceeds of one Saturday and Sunday night to the fund."

He dropped a chunk of *panela* into his cup and stirred.

"The word got around that the money for those two nights would go for the plaza and she did a land-office business. It turned into sort of a fiesta and what with all the gay spirits and drinking the crowd broke up some of her furniture."

He grinned, remembering. "She came to see me

Monday morning. She was furious. She asked, 'Who's going to pay for my furniture?' I put her off but she tattled to the priest when she took her donation. She told Father 'It's all the fault of the gringo.'"

"Does Padre Ortiz know how she makes her money?"

He nodded. "He's stuck with her the same way I am. She's part of this town and we're trying to get her to take some responsibility for its welfare. Padre told her it was very generous of her to donate but he didn't offer to give back any of her money to replace the furniture."

The Peace Corps, like politicians, seemed to have some strange affiliations.

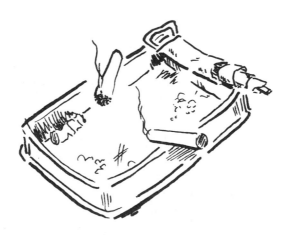

Several afternoons later Richard and his housemates burst through the front door, exhuberant with excitement. There was much back-slapping and joking with Richard taking the brunt of the teasing. When Mario and Albero left they were still calling remarks over their shoulders.

"What was that about?"

Richard was laughing so hard he couldn't answer for a minute or two. When he regained control he told a tale.

"The Madam sent me a message today."

"Oh?"

"She sent word she was ready to have a baby with me." An explosion of laughter rocked him.

I thought I'd misunderstood. "What?"

"You heard me right. She's looked you over and you suit her. Now we can have a baby together, your grandchild."

A smirking face awaited my reaction. The invitation stunned me.

"She says for me to come down tonight and then when you go back to the States she will go with you."

Through snorts and cackles he pictured my homecoming.

"Just think how lovely it will be. You can give a tea and introduce her to all your friends. You can say she's a very successful businesswoman. Then, if you ever want to retire, she can open a house and support you in a manner to which you are unaccustomed."

He wiped mirth-teared eyes. For some reason he found the situation excruciatingly funny.

"Now that's class! You've been chosen as a mother-in-law. It's the chance of a lifetime!"

Somehow I couldn't warm up to the opportunity. I'll admit it's the only proposition of its kind I've ever had.

When his hilarity had subsided Richard commented with some seriousness, "It's really quite a concession."

"Concession?"

"Remember the broken furniture. Her offer means I am forgiven."

"Congratulations." He missed the sarcasm.

"Of course, when you leave town without her she'll know we turned her down. I'll have to dream up some story that won't hurt her feelings."

"Why? What possible difference could it make?"

His eyebrows raised at my lack of perception.

"She's somebody in this town."

"Who?"

"A woman of position."

Just what that position was I've never really known.

Silently he mulled over the prospects of soothing the Madam's hurt feelings. I washed the dishes and got into bed, scooting under the covers to read. Suddenly I remembered the boisterous homecoming of the boys.

"Did Mario and Albero know about the Madam's offer?"

"Yes. They were pointing out all the advantages of having a Madam in the family."

Later, when he slid into his sleeping bag he snickered.

"Just think of the sacrifice I'm making for you!"

"What sacrifice?"

"Why, if I weren't behaving so respectably because you are visiting me," he paused to leer suggestively, "I could be down at the Zone collecting my reward!"

"Don't let me cramp your style!"

"I'm not. It's a pleasure to forego this attractive opportunity in honor of my dear, respected mother's visit," he parodied in flowery imitation of local courtesies.

I gave him an icy look. Too well I knew this remark was only the beginning. For the rest of my life I'd hear versions of this tale repeated at the worst possible moments.

14
La Palanca

"There's no easy way to make a change," Richard complained. "Whenever I want to improve something every person asks 'what will I get out of it?' before he will move a muscle. Everything has to be done with *palanca*."

Imagining a harvest months away must be a vague concept to people accustomed to thinking only as far as the next meal. The long-range advantages of animal feeding programs and better sanitation would be even hazier.

"Before I suggest an idea I have to know what to answer to their objections. It strains my brain."

But he utilized every scrap of information he possessed to accomplish his purposes, a fact which became annoyingly clear the day I tackled the laundry. Our house was well-equipped to wash.

We had soap, we had water, and we had Mistrató's marvellous answer to the washing machine, all handily combined under one roof. The washing machine was a hollow block of concrete some 30 inches high, a normal waist-height for a Colombian woman but a back-breaking level for me. The faucet hung above this block.

Beside it stood another cement block with a slanted top of very rough concrete. It had already been explained that this breathtakingly modern convenience was vastly superior to the old laundry method. Formerly, one carried the clothes to the river and stood ankle-deep in water while washing them.

The women of Mistrató do not rub clothes; they slap the dirt free. The rough texture of the slab aids in loosening the soil. So I wet a garment under the faucet, rubbed on soap, and slapped.

Suds flew in every direction. I stopped to glance across the fence. The neighbor washing in the next yard didn't have this problem. Maybe there was too much soap.

I rinsed out some of the suds and began slapping again. Nothing happened except the fabric started to show signs of wear from my energetic beating. While I slapped and experimented, eventually returning to my own hand-rubbing methods, the woman next door hung out piece after piece of dazzling laundry, draping them on the fence and bushes to dry in the noonday sun. My house had a clothesline but only two pieces flapped on it when my neighbor finished her wash.

There was no point in inquiring about her wonderful detergent. I needed to ask her to show me how to wash.

After two more hours of vigorous effort my line was full, and I was disgustedly surveying the results of my labors when the front door opened.

"We have an invitation," Richard announced as he came through the house and out onto the porch. He glanced at the laundry. "Looks pretty good."

"By tonight everyone in town will know the gringo's mother doesn't know how to wash." With those streaked clothes snapping in the breeze how could anyone think otherwise.

"You'll do better next time."

There wouldn't be any next time if I could prevent it.

Richard went back to his news. "We've been invited to a seance."

Articles I'd read suggested that people in primitive areas were often accomplished in the occult. Richard had been angling for an invitation from a small circle of people pursuing such activities but the group was suspicious. Today he'd finally managed it.

"How did you do it?"

"Oh, I told them you could dowse."

"You didn't!"

Dowsing was a slight ability I'd chanced upon when I imitated a plumber locating underground pipes with the method. I didn't brag about it to my friends since I didn't know how to explain it. Privately I'd thought it to be an unknown law of static electricity. It was difficult to make this delicate point in English. It would be impossible in Spanish.

"It was the lever that got us invited. They think you

have magic and they want to meet you."

I wished he'd been able to get the invitation some other way but the opportunity to attend a seance in the Andes was not easily come by.

We hurried through the evening meal and set out for the address. The few people awaiting our arrival in the tiny living room greeted me with curiosity. After about thirty minutes of amenities we were led to a small back room. The windows were boarded up, sealing it from outside eyes. A horseshoe of chairs was closed by a small table covered with a white cotton cloth. In the center was a tiny, white satin pillow.

The group seated themselves in the chairs and one man who had spoken only when introduced seated himself at the table. He was Efraín Branadú, the medium, a stocky man beginning to grey at the temples and dressed in work clothes. In the normal lighting of the room heads were bowed and Mr. Branadú offered a prayer.

It was an extraordinary prayer. A blessing was asked on this gathering who wished in no way to offend the Catholic church. Protection was requested from demons who might wish to enter the group. A petition was made for spirits having an interest in anyone in the group to attend the meeting. There was a short silence when the prayer was finished.

The medium kept his eyes closed. His hands began a rhythmic patting on the pillow. A pallor seemed to whiten his face. The patting became thumps. A moment later his hands stretched rigidly on the cushion, and then slowly relaxed. With his eyes still closed he began speaking.

FOURTEEN

A smooth flow of words issued from his lips. The group listened intently, glancing from time to time at Richard and me. After several minutes the spokesman for the group leaned toward Richard.

"He gives you messages in English, doesn't he?"

Richard shook his head. "That's not English. Don't you understand the language either?"

His statement caused a hushed flurry of consulting. No one understood the medium's words. The spokesman interrupted the medium.

"Will you please ask the spirits to speak in English or Spanish. No one here can translate your words."

The medium finished what sounded like a sentence before lapsing into silence. Several minutes passed. When he began speaking again it was in excellent Spanish, much different from the usual vocabulary of Mistrató. These words were directed to Richard and me and purported to be messages from his father. After speaking for several minutes the medium again became silent.

Now the group directed questions to the spirits. One member wished to find a lost article. A woman wanted to know if her father would recover from his illness. A man requested advice on a small business venture. The fact the group was asking such questions indicated previous answers must have been given that proved accurate. It seemed the same spirits did not answer all questions, but shared the honors. After the better part of two hours the meeting ended and we returned to the living room to discuss it.

"Are you pleased with the messages?" someone asked me.

Only one fact in the messages had been a startling approach to the truth of a private matter, a fact which could have been picked up telepathically, but we expressed our appreciation anyway.

"Then will you do a favor for us?"

"But of course."

"We want you to find something underground."

Their eyes impaled me. "I've found only pipes or water," I objected lamely.

"But you will do this thing for us?"

How could I refuse?

"I'll try. It may not work in the mountains."

"Describe what you need."

I told of the two short lengths of copper wire bent into L shapes. As soon as they understood, a man in the group departed to locate the wire. The group chatted about their psychic experiences during his absence. In a little while the man came back with the copper wire, electric wiring stripped of insulation. We were going to do this experiment in the dark!

Two men and one woman rose to accompany us. As we straggled down the street to a vacant lot almost overgrown by brush I worried aloud to Richard.

"What if it doesn't work?"

"You left yourself an out."

But I was sure this minor talent so calmly taken for granted would desert me now that I was asked to demonstrate and I'd be left with egg on my face.

Guided by Richard's flashlight we crashed through bushes and weeds, lurching over uneven ground that smelled oddly of decay and mold, to a small clearing where the medium stopped. He pointed to a spot beneath the tree.

"Try here."

Obediently I grasped the short ends of the L-shaped wires, braced them against my collar bones and walked slowly forward. Nothing happened.

Moving over from the indicated spot I tried again, walking a parallel line with the first course. Near the designated spot the wires swung together making a perfect X. A path two feet away produced no signal. I tried a right-angle course to the point where the wires had crossed. They crossed again.

"Here," I pointed. A stake was driven in the ground to mark the spot.

Several more times I went through the same routine, once again in the same field and then in another place which appeared to be an abandoned cemetery. At the end of an hour there were three stakes driven in the ground.

A few times the two men had taken the wires from my hands to see if they could produce the same results. The medium could, but the spokesman, even with cheating, couldn't get a strong signal.

On the way home I worried about the outcome.

"They probably won't find anything."

"It doesn't matter. You tried."

As we were getting ready for bed we discussed the evening. Richard mentioned the peculiar incident of the unknown tongue.

"I wish we'd had a tape recorder. Then we could have taken the tape to a linguist. It might have been a language and then again it might have been gibberish. It sounded a little like Catio."

"Is that a language?"

"Yes, but it's dying out. The Indians in the rain forest speak it. I've heard it a time or two on market day but I can't remember it well enough to identify it."

"How could the medium have learned it?"

"That's the point. He couldn't. He was born and raised here. You should see him try to write his own name. There is no possibility he could have mastered Catio to speak it so smoothly."

If Richard was right, we'd missed an interesting opportunity to verify an unknown language coming from the medium's lips. The fluent cultured Spanish in the messages to Richard and me had been a curious facet of the seance, too.

But the seance was gone from my mind when Richard came in very late the next night, plastered to his knees with mud and carrying his cherished case of garden tools. He washed the spade and fork and cleaned the handles while I watched.

"What have you been doing?"

"Digging." He sounded grumpy.

"I can see that, but where?"

"Where you pointed."

"Did you find anything?"

"Yep." He was in a bad humor and was going to make me drag the information out of him.

"Is it a secret or can you tell me what you found?"

"Water!" he exploded, "in every damn place you

pointed. Mistrató has three new wells, if it wants them!

"Why are you so angry?"

"They weren't looking for water or pipes. They were looking for gold."

"Gold!"

Suddenly the intrigue was transparent. If the mother could locate pipes or water then maybe she could locate gold. No wonder we'd been so welcome.

"Those places they showed you are supposed to be the sites of buried treasure."

"But if they knew where the treasure was likely to be, why didn't they dig and find out?"

"Digging is work, and only the gringo works. Who do you suppose dug tonight and got all muddy?"

I burst into laughter. Their plan had been so hilariously successful. Even after hearing the running conversations about buried treasure, Richard had been talked into doing the digging after his mother had been drafted to verify the sites. Sorry as I was for Richard's discomfiture I couldn't restrain my amusement.

"Oh, well, it will give them a new hobby," he decided. "They'll be running all over the mountains for years looking for gold."

"Do you think there is any gold in these mountains?"

"None that I know of. There's platinum, though. The geological survey several years ago showed platinum deposits but nobody can pinpoint the location."

Unexpectedly he chuckled. "Wouldn't it be funny if someone did locate the platinum with those wires. The town would be rich. They might even put up a statue of you."

It didn't seem a reasonable expectation. It was more likely that after abandoning the magic of the wires they would set about hatching another plot and persuade some geologist to verify hopeful sites. Whatever they devised it was certain the plan wouldn't include doing any of the actual work. That role would be performed by another unsuspecting person.

It shouldn't be too difficult to dream up a new angle. After all, it was only a matter of finding the right *palanca*.

15
Strange Solutions

A charcoal gray mouse flattened its body and slid up through a crack in the floor. A moment later it streaked up the table leg and scampered among the food containers, hunting one accidentally left open. Just one more problem in Mistrató that had no easy remedy.

Richard and I had discussed the mice earlier.

"There's no such thing as mouse traps. We need to buy a cat."

"Buy?" I'd been battling gifts of free kittens since the children were born.

"Yeah. People sell them on market day. Nobody gives you an animal, even if it's half-dead, and all the cats look like they're on their ninth lives."

"Aren't any of the cats fat?" I remembered the dreadful thinness of the one at market.

"I've never seen a fat one. Maybe the people eat them. The ones for sale look so sick I worry all the time about rabies."

Where I lived in the States it was difficult to get the population to vaccinate their animals for rabies. It was to be expected the problem would be multiplied here.

"The people don't even vaccinate their children for anything. I'm just now teaching the farmers how to inoculate against a few animal diseases." He shrugged. "It's really just a matter of deciding whether you want to put up with the mice or worry about rabies." He was offering me a choice.

"I'll settle for the mice."

"They aren't too bad a nuisance. You have to remember to keep the food tightly covered, but mice don't get in bed with you. Now when we had roaches, that was another thing! It was very exciting!"

"Exciting?" Pictures of Richard and his housemates spraying with insecticide passed through my head, hardly a vision to elate anyone.

"Yeah, you see, we had to buy chickens. For some reason this house had become infested with cockroaches, an army of them. None of the other houses on the block had them and I never did know why. We killed dozens of the two- or three-inch-long size but the minute the light went out at night a million more crawled out of the walls and traipsed over everything, including us. We were hopping out of bed all night, shaking the covers and killing the ones we could catch."

I readjusted my vision of insecticide sprays.

"So we bought some chickens and kept them inside the house. The first few nights they nearly scared us out of our wits, flapping down from their roosts and diving on the roaches. All night long they squawked and flounced around, sometimes landing on us if they spied a roach in the bed. In a couple of weeks, there wasn't a roach left."

"But didn't the chickens make a mess?"

"A little, but we scrubbed the floors every couple of days and it wasn't too bad."

"What happened to the chickens after you got rid of the roaches?"

"I bought out Mario and Albero's interest and now I keep the chickens at Doña Albertina's. That's why we had eggs when we ate there."

It fit in with a remark he'd made one day when he was digging everything I'd discarded out of the wastebasket.

"You mustn't waste. You're throwing away good things!" His hands smoothed the paper tissue from my new stockings. A tuna fish can was carefully lifted out and an empty tissue box joined the things he saved.

"Why do you want that trash?"

"It isn't trash. The tissue is for toilet paper. The can will make an ashtray and I'll use the tissue box to carry medicines." The wastebasket was nearly empty.

"What about cigarette butts?" Surely he couldn't find a use for those.

"Throw them out in the corral. The chickens from next door will eat them."

It was all perfectly logical. Horses ate spaghetti, people took no notice of worms, so why shouldn't chickens eat tobacco? Maybe, as Richard suggested, the people even ate the fat cats! The gray meat on my plate at Doña Albertina's flashed through my head. Richard had consistently refused to discuss the origin of that meat. I shuddered at this new possibility. Mistratóans found a number of foods—if that is what you would call them— appetizing that didn't strike one spark of enthusiasm in me.

The fact that they could eat the slimy, fish-colored meat displayed at market was an enigma. They were satisfied, even pleased, with the selection. Albero was the exception, but then Albero's mind was beginning to flex its muscles. Richard had inspired him with the concept of a better life.

And Albero's assistance in implementing the dream brought him vexing decisions. He was the first sanitation inspector the town had ever employed. It was his responsibility to supervise the slaughterhouse, making certain that sanitary methods were followed in the butchering. But before the butchering he had the dangerous authority of deciding whether the animal brought for slaughter was healthy enough to be used for food. Sometimes the verdict had to be made almost by intuition.

The small farmer had quickly learned the advantage of penicillin which was available without prescription. He knew massive doses would keep an animal alive long enough to get it to the abattoir. The slaughter frequently barely preceded the time when the animal would have succumbed from disease. Formerly, with no inspection,

the diseased meat was offered for purchase by an unconcerned public.

With the backing of the city fathers, Richard was
able to get an ordinance requiring an animal to be delivered to the killing floor at least eighteen hours before
time for slaughter. This delay allowed time for any medication to wear off and disease to be detected. At first
Richard inspected, but his other duties made it impossible
for him to be present every butchering day, so Albero
was appointed.

Although Albero had no training for the job, Richard
was able to teach him the major signs of disease, but he
was in a quandary when unusual symptoms appeared. In
this eventuality the rule was that the hide and viscera of
the animal were to be saved until Richard could inspect it,
but as one might expect, the offal mysteriously disappeared only too often. It was one of these quandaries
which brought Albero home early one afternoon looking
for Richard.

I told him Richard was in the mountains.

"When will he be home?"

"Maybe by four o'clock, maybe not." I was becoming
as indefinite as everyone around me.

"When he comes, tell him to meet me at the market.
I have trouble."

Without remembering his goodbyes, he rushed away.
Shortly afterward Richard returned. He, too, left in a
hurry after my message. An hour later they came back
together, deep in discussion.

"What was the trouble?"

Between them they described the riddle of the dripping meat.

"For two hours water ran out of the meat. It looked very peculiar," Albero reported.

"Edema, or dropsy," Richard decided. "I don't know whether it was dangerous after cooking but I condemned it."

"And when we went back to the slaughterhouse the hide and viscera were gone," Albero added.

"Nobody knew where they went, of course," Richard said, "but the farmer was furious when I rejected the meat anyway."

"What happens now?"

"The police watch while the farmer takes all the meat and burns it. Then he has to scrub his stand where the meat was displayed. The owner blames Albero because he wouldn't let him sell any of the meat until I saw it. Albero won't be safe until the farmer leaves town."

"I'm planning a quiet evening at home," Albero grinned.

The precarious position Albero occupied was not to be envied. When he rejected an animal he was removing an essential source of yearly income from a poor farmer whose children might starve as the result of his decree. He was fully aware of this aspect of the situation and each condemnation was accompanied by soul-searching. Although Albero tried to make light of these inner anxieties Richard and I were both aware of his anguish.

"He does his job but he bleeds," Richard commented after Albero had trudged away to supervise the final disposition of the meat.

In between those miserable times when Albero felt forced to condemn, his mind was expanding. Some of his muddles he'd begun to settle in his own way. Richard told me about one.

"Albero can read well and so I showed him the pictures of bacteria in my animal science books. He believes he could see these things under a microscope. As soon as he understood about germs he began to worry. On market day he begged people to keep the meat off the ground so dogs and cats couldn't chew on it. Of course, nobody paid any attention to him.'

Richard smiled, remembering Albero's frustration.

"He didn't go to the priest, as I would have, and get him to announce a new rule over the speaker. Albero settled the impasse himself. On the next market day he bought some meat, cut it up into small pieces and doused them with strychnine. Then he toured the market handing out morsels to every dog he saw. It sure was rough on the dog population but Albero decided people were more important than dogs."

"What was said when so many dogs died?"

"Not a blasted word! A sudden demise of dozens of dogs, practically a town event, and not one person mentioned it to either of us. They knew what had happened. But the next market day there wasn't a dog in sight. They were tied up at home."

A laugh rumbled from his throat. "Albero made one little mistake. He didn't pay enough attention to whose dog it was he was feeding. He handed one of his choice morsels to his fiancée's dog by mistake and her dog died too. That's why his love affair is having so many bumps. She's mad at him yet over it."

Distractedly I thought about the cruelty of Albero's solution as I scratched my stomach. I was scratching the way everyone else did in Mistrató. It must be the combination of harsh soap and local water causing the itching. I said as much to Richard. His eyes widened.

"Let me see."

I unbuttoned my blouse to show him the rash on my middle.

"You've got *chinches*," he guffawed.

"What's that?"

"Bedbugs!" He knelt to open the foot locker. Removing a shaker can he moved to the bed and dusted a generous sprinkling on the sheets and pillow, rubbing it in vigorously.

"Everybody has bedbugs," he tossed over his shoulder. "I fight them all the time."

This wasn't the first time I'd seen the shaker can. He'd dusted it into his sleeping bag several nights ago. At the time I'd thought it a nicety of preferring to smell bath powder rather than the rank odor of the bag. But as the odor rose in the air, I identified the strange odor of my bed I'd noticed the first night. He must have treated the bed before my arrival.

"What is that powder, antiseptic?"

"D.D.T. It kills them off for a few days."

I wondered if breathing it would kill me too but it was only a hazy concern.

"All the problems here have remedies. They're just not the same remedies you're used to," Richard consoled. "Generally they're about as effective though."

The D.D.T. worked. If I had some bad moments at night thinking about what happened to people coated with the poison, they were as nothing compared to my horror of sleeping with bedbugs. Mistrató had many solutions, as Richard said, but there were a few I could have willingly dispensed with learning.

16
An Oasis

During the first days in Mistrató I met two ladies who proved to be lifesavers. They operated the only soft-goods store in town. The filthy beach towel Richard thought I should use for everything had become a bone of contention.

"Four people cannot use the same towel and expect to be clean." I was adamant, irked by such idiocy.

"Well, O.K. I'll show you where to buy some towels but don't get the finest. Get the cheapest they have."

He took me to a store I'd noticed but had never entered. It had a raised floor and one climbed two steps to its door. Very likely it was the only business in town not flooded when the rains came each year. Our approach was watched and when we stepped through the door two ladies standing behind the counters came forward to greet us. These were the Gallones sisters.

Both were dark-haired women in their early thirties. Blanca, a small, vivacious person, was beautiful. Long silky hair, done in a flip, barely touched her shoulders. Heavily lashed dark eyes set off the apricot color of her skin. Amalia, slightly larger, and the older of the two, was very attractive too but lacked the volatility of the younger woman. Amalia wore her hair short, neatly styled with soft waves on either side of her face.

The Gallones were as well-dressed as any business people from larger cities, with hose, heels, and deftly-applied make-up. Instead of doing business, the ladies immediately locked up the store upon our arrival and we trooped upstairs to their apartment. A tray appeared carrying chilled soft drinks. Richard sipped his soda but when he saw the immediate rapport between us he finished it quickly and made excuses to leave.

From the minute we met I felt I'd known Blanca and Amalia forever. When they discovered I'd been in the ready-to-wear business it was a further bond. They asked about my shop and we compared merchandise. My house came up for discussion—the electric appliances and heating equipment. When all questions were answered they showed me their apartment.

The furniture was similar to the type used in weekend homes, sturdy wood frames, plastic upholstery, and done in bright shades of orange and blue. There were vanity tables in the bedrooms and beds with innerspring mattresses. The kitchen was equally attractive.

In addition to cabinets, a plastic-topped table and a sink, it had an apartment-size electric stove, a fact unknown to Richard. The Gallones could produce biscuits and cornbread from the local, rough cornmeal and a fairly palatable bread. Their bread wasn't the two-inch-high sagging loaf I'd become accustomed to. It was nearly as high as an American loaf because the Gallones used yeast in their recipe. It tasted similar to cracked wheat bread but slightly sweeter. They stored their baked goods in built-in wall cabinets. There was one tall cabinet which contained several dozen cans of food.

Tins of tomato paste, mangos, milk, pineapple, and canned meat from Argentina stood in neat rows beside tightly capped glass jars of rice, beans, white sugar, and packets of plastic-wrapped cookies. Blanca removed a packet for each of us while they told me about their meals. I was surprised at the supply of canned goods and inquired where they'd purchased it.

"Anserma," Amalia replied. "Once a month we go to Anserma and select what we need. The first truck coming here to pick up plátano, avocados, or some other product brings our groceries to us. Where did you get your food supply?"

At my answer that Richard had none, the ladies looked silently at each other, too polite to show their dismay. They recovered quickly though and went on talking about the food.

"Other things we buy here, such as fresh vegetables in season, or dried products such as beans and rice. Our little boy does the shopping," Blanca concluded.

I'd been given to understand the ladies were single. "You have a little brother?"

"No, no," they both laughed as a comment flipped between them. "The boy for the groceries."

Amalia held up one finger. "Let me explain. A little boy comes every day to see if we need anything. We tell him what we want and he runs around to the little farms near town and buys produce for us. For example, tomatoes, oranges, avocados, and bananas are in season. When he returns with the food the girl for the plates washes everything and stores what needs to be chilled in the refrigerator."

I hadn't seen the refrigerator although there had to be one. The drinks were chilled. Later I saw that the electric refrigerator was on the ground floor inside a storeroom. It had been too heavy for anyone in town to bring up to the second floor.

By the standards of Mistrató the Gallones lived quite well. To live in this manner, it seemed, it was necessary to have a boy for the horse, a boy for the groceries, and a girl for the plates, and the girl for the plates had many duties besides that of washing dishes.

The energetic young lady who worked for the Gallones was sweeping the walk in the flower garden behind the house when we descended to make my purchases.

Dishtowels, I discovered, were bought by the yard. I purchased three yards, intending to tear the fabric into three pieces, leaving them rough-edged. The little maid came at once and took the fabric from Blanca, disappearing into the back of the store. Before I finished selecting

bathtowels and washrags she was back with four dishtowels, neatly hemmed and even equipped with a small
loop on the corner of each which would fit over a nail.

When I inquired about the charge for the sewing I
was told there was none—that it was a favor. I paid for my
purchases, mentally calculating the exchange rate. The
bathtowels cost fifteen cents each, the washrags three
cents each, and the four dishtowels had amounted to five
cents per towel. The visit and the purchases had taken
longer than I thought and when I left I'd spent two hours
in the company of the Gallones.

But on the way home my spirit was light. I had found
two friends to whom I could turn. The private school
educations of Amalia and Blanca had amounted to eleven
years and when they had regretfully returned to live in
Mistrató upon the death of their father they'd been iso-
lated from nearly everything they'd learned to enjoy.

With no men in town of equal education, the years
ahead loomed manless for Amalia and Blanca. I had gotten
the impression that they didn't visit in the homes of
Mistrató to any extent either and their promise to visit
me as we parted I'd taken as a courtesy not to be kept.
They surprised me by visiting Richard's house that same
evening.

I conducted them through the house, as they had
shown me theirs, and when the tour was over a serious
conversation in low tones took place between them. Their
nods told me they'd agreed on something.

Blanca took my hands. "You must pack up and move
in with us immediately. This is a peasant's house and not

what you are used to at home."

I was astonished and touched. I thanked them but went on to explain why I dare not leave Richard's house. I told of his pledge to live on the peasant level while he worked in Mistrató.

"Did you make this promise too?" Amalia wanted to know.

"I promised Richard I would do nothing to jeopardize his work."

The sisters stared thoughtfully at each other.

"At least come to our house for your bath and meals," Blanca insisted. "Let me do your hair whenever you want to wash it. I have pins and rollers and everything to do our hair. It will be a pleasure to do yours."

Their sympathy and kindness were turning my insides to jelly but again I tried to explain the breadth of Richard's commitment.

"If I do anything that Richard does not do the people will say, 'The gringo has hidden wealth. See—his mother needs luxuries.' He might lose his effectiveness because I chose to be comfortable."

There was another thoughtful silence before they agreed with me.

"Yes, the peasants are ignorant. They believe many foolish things," Amalia said.

The talk moved to other things and we spent another interesting hour together. Later that week I heard they had told a customer about me.

"The gringo's mothers is also very religious. Both are really missionaries in spite of a confusion by the United

States government in calling them something else. They are heroic people."

Heroic was the last adjective I could have expected. Inefficient was the word that fit me. On subsequent visits with the Gallones I dropped in and sat on a stool in the store while we visited. With the aid of a Spanish-English dictionary they owned we talked of a multitude of things.

One thing they mentioned was their lack of companionship. The only women they counted as friends were the sisters of the priest and Mrs. Vallejo, the doctor's wife.

"Most of the town thinks we are very rich," Amalia said. "Our visit to one of the homes would be regarded with hostility. It would be most uncomfortable for everyone. You have a word for it in America, the visiting of the people who live in squalor."

"Slumming?"

The sisters looked at each other, testing the word on their tongues before they nodded agreement.

"And even if this attitude did not exist they're so dirty we'd be afraid to eat anything they served as refreshments," Blanca added.

"Their conversation is all gossip, about which one did what. You've probably noticed they watch every thing you do. You've stimulated the conversation all over town."

I knew I was the newest local attraction.

"And they're so lazy. The girl for the plates is the only girl in town who is brisk. She wasn't when she came but little by little she got used to our ways," Amalia added.

Silently I decided that the girl for the plates was eating a better diet than ever before in her life and was probably in better health. There was something other than a language barrier between the Gallones and the rest of the townspeople. The ladies lived in the midst of starvation, not even comprehending it.

On another visit we'd talked about my disaster with the laundry. They laughed until tears came into their eyes and consoled me with pats.

"Your sheets, towels, and pillowcases you must send to a laundress. Do all your nice things yourself in the basin."

The laundress they recommended turned out to be a woman with exactly the same laundry facilities I had but she knew what to do with them. From then on I took the linens to her.

Once we discussed the operation of a small store in the United States. I described the fixtures and stock I had carried and both women nodded in understanding.

"The same as in Bogotá. They carry only ready-made clothes and have air conditioning."

"But here, our sales are mostly fabrics which the women stitch up at home. Shoes are the only other thing that sells in quantity." Blanca reached over to take down a shoe box and remove a shoe. "The quality is very poor, but then the price is cheap too."

I felt the leather, if it was leather. Paper thin and stiff. It was a very small size. I peered inside to discern the numbers but they were blurred.

"How many sizes do you stock?"

"Four sizes, in medium and wide widths." They listed the sizes which are different from in the States. Translated the sizes were from four to seven, but very few in sevens.

"How about the sizes in mens' shoes?"

"The same."

Blanca looked down at my 8AAAA foot and giggled. "In this town you would have to go barefoot."

I glanced at their shoes, high-heeled, patent and not only very small but narrow. They caught my look.

"Bogotá. We go twice a year to spend a few days to shop. We buy several pairs at one time," Amalia answered. She reached to feel my purse. "Leather?"

"Foam plastic."

They took the bag on their laps and felt it carefully. I explained it was possible to wipe off smears with a damp cloth. With my nod of permission they opened it, looking at all the pockets and zippers inside.

"How much would this cost Colombian?"

"About three dollars."

"Could you send each of us one exactly like it?"

It was news to them that their own customs department had such a long list of forbidden importations. At their disappointment I asked if they didn't see the same products when they went to their seasonal markets. They didn't go to market. Their wants were satisfied by salesmen who came to see them about once a year.

"But Colombia has a very flourishing plastic industry. It is likely you can get the same purse here and for less money. When you go to Bogotá next time ask in the small shops for women about where they buy their purses. Someone will know."

"But of course! Bogotá already had shoes in colored plastic the last time we were there. Perhaps by our next visit there will be handbags too," Amalia agreed.

For several visits I'd been aware, peripherally, that Blanca's and Amalia's floors were different from the others in town. They fit as tightly as hardwood floors. Every other floor in town had cracks through which the mice came to visit. There were no rugs in Mistrató so the floor faults were immediately visible to anyone entering the house. But the Gallones floors not only fit perfectly, they appeared to be of polished cherry. One day I remembered to ask about them.

"The wood to build with in Mistrató is not cured," Amalia told me. "After one year the boards shrink and dry. It is necessary to take up the whole floor and add more boards when it is nailed down again. The peasants don't bother to go to all this trouble." She pointed to a corner of the flower garden behind the house where a few dozen 1 x 4 boards leaned against the fence.

"Those boards have been curing for several years. Whenever we need wood we use that lumber, replacing whatever we use with new raw boards which can cure until we need to make other repairs."

"But how did you get this lovely color? Is it stain or varnish?"

"Oh, the color just happens in the cleaning of the floors. We use no added color on them," Blanca said.

"Unfinished wood at home simply gets whiter and more weatherbeaten from mopping," I objected.

"Not mopping." Blanca jumped off her stool and

went into the storeroom to return with a large wad of the Colombian counterpart of steel wool. "Lemon oil and this cleans our floors."

"Like this?" I made a scrubbing motion.

"No," Blanca laughed, "like this."

She dropped the rough, loosely-rolled material on the floor, put her foot on it and scuffled around the floor.

"The girl for the plates puts one under each foot when she cleans our floors," Amalia explained.

Did the girl for the plates have a secret skill of pointing her toes to get in the corners too? I wished I'd been able to witness the feat!

Before I left Mistrató I went alone to make my final call. In my improving Spanish I told them what their friendship had meant to me. Tears came in their eyes.

At my little gift of a vial of perfume for each, Amalia put her arms around me.

"Promise you will return, but not to live as Richard lives. We will help you arrange things so you can live well, and then we will make trips together to Bogotá."

I hugged Amalia in return.

"It is a long and expensive trip. I doubt if I can make the trip again. Why don't you and Blanca plan to visit me in the United States?"

Blanca's eyes brightened with enthusiasm.

"Why not?" She turned to Amalia. "We can plan for it and in a few years we can go to visit our friend." She was anticipating the trip already.

I gave Blanca a leave-taking hug.

"I will write to you. As your plans are made let me

know so I can arrange sight-seeing trips for you."

When we parted I wiped away a few tears, knowing the chance they could make the journey was slight. They would have to sell thousands of yards of fabric and hundreds of pairs of shoes to finance the trip. I was leaving two friends in Mistrató, and although we still stumbled over the language there was empathy between us. We were *simpático*.

The Gallones had been the oasis in a desert of strange customs and misunderstandings. Richard's Peace Corps protocol list had not included any women. Without doubt, being male he was provided with male contacts. A girl Volunteer working in Mistrató might have been given a different list, including Blanca and Amalia. Richard had fled to Padre Ortiz and Dr. Vallejo when his problems piled up faster than his solutions, for these men spoke his language.

Blanca and Amalia had spoken mine.

17
The City Doctor

On the day before my plane was to leave Bogotá we began the tortuous trip back to civilization, jolting along recklessly in another ancient conveyance over the fearsome mountain road. All obstacles had been surmounted and we were approaching Anserma when Richard took a notebook from his pocket.

"I have to see Dr. Ramírez, the Vet. His office is here."

"Will there be time?"

"You don't have to catch the feeder plane from Pereira until tomorrow morning."

The taxi deposited us in front of the bus station. Eight more people disembarked, two of whom had been picked up along the road and had stood on the back bumpers, clinging happily to the trunk latches. We crossed the street and passed several stores before Richard turned into an entrance.

Eggs, seeds, block salt, animal feed, medicines, chickens, and everything else one expects to find in a farm supply house jammed the room. A young man peered out of an inner office when he heard Richard's shout. As soon as he saw us he rushed out.

Dr. Ramírez was a blond, blue-eyed, stockily-built young man, possibly thirty years old. He clicked his heels in a manner reminiscent of the German military when he was introduced. He was delighted that Richard had brought me to meet him and immediately made plans to take us to lunch.

While he was giving instructions to his two employees Richard explained the store.

"Anserma asked Dr. Ramírez to locate here. But whenever he prescribed medicine or planned a feeding program the products required were not available. He tried to persuade other merchants to stock what he needed but no one would invest the money. So he borrowed and slowly equipped this store. Now he has a good business in addition to his medical work. That's what he wants me to do in Mistrató."

The young man had finished his instructions and was donning his coat.

"But I talked the drugstores in Mistrató into carrying the medicines. Dr. Ramírez used to come every month to Mistrató but since I've been there he's stopped making the trip. I do all the animal work for the area. If I have an animal I'm worried about, I come to Anserma to talk with him about it."

The doctor rejoined us and announced our schedule.

"First we must have an iced drink and get acquainted. Then we will discuss Richard's animals."

He led the way to a small coffee shop. The iced drink turned out to be a Coke taken directly from an electric refrigerator. We chatted as the icy sweetness slipped down my throat. Richard took out his list again.

As his finger inched down the paper with each answer from the doctor, twice there was a disagreement. Richard pencilled a mark beside these jottings. When he reached the end of the reminders we headed back to the feed store.

"We will look in the medical books," Dr. Ramírez said.

We entered the inner office. The room contained an unexpected number of books, including a number of volumes whose titles were in German. Each man scanned the shelves and took down one book, leafing through it to find a reference.

A spirited discussion followed. While one man pointed to a paragraph, he was disputed by the other who trained a finger on the passage he was quoting. There must have been a slight language difficulty for occasionally Richard would use an English medical term. Dr. Ramírez would repeat it and then translate it into German. It was slightly befuddling to hear Richard argue from a Spanish textbook while Dr. Ramírez quoted from a German manual.

Finally, to eliminate the misunderstanding they drew pictures of the disorders they were debating. The disagreement was then very quickly settled. The veterinarian wrote two formulas which Richard copied and with their arms about each other's shoulders they announced they were ready for lunch.

"We'll go to my club to eat," Dr. Ramírez told us as he pulled his Japanese jeep away from its parking place.

The jeep was new and sped along the widening road. We were traveling a different route from the one the bus had taken when we arrived. Instead of lush slopes of jungle, this land was nearly all under cultivation. Broad expanses of furrowed rows squeezed small sections of untamed jungle between them. Occasionally we passed a tractor working in a field. Several lovely homes dotted the landscape, too far back from the road for close inspection. For an hour we traveled past increasingly modernized agriculture before our host turned off the highway.

He followed a road leading to a long, low cement building fronted by a swimming pool. A few adults and a bevy of children were swimming, and about thirty other people were inside the open-fronted clubhouse, eating or dancing to a raucously amplified jukebox. The interior of the building was ultra-modern, utilizing large panes of glass and plastic.

As soon as we were seated at a small glass table the waiter brought three frosty bottles of beer instead of water. Dr. Ramírez ordered our lunch, giving precise instructions.

"The club has just been finished," the doctor said. "The farmers in this area are prospering and for the first time they have money. Their families shop in Bogotá, flying in for a few days vacation and shopping several times a year."

His words explained the smart play clothes everyone wore.

"Several of the farmers got together and decided to build the club. They were nice enough to invite me to be one of the charter members although I am poor compared to their new standards." His eyes turned to Richard's. "I wanted you to see how nice the life could be with a little money."

"It's beautiful, but I couldn't afford to eat here, let

alone become a member."

"That's exactly the point. I have less than most of these farmers, but you have nothing, and it's your own fault."

While Dr. Ramírez was talking two girls were scrutinizing our table. They were clearly trying to decide which man was my escort. They must have chosen the doctor for a moment later Richard was treated to flirting from both. Soon he went to dance with one of them.

When he left the table Dr. Ramírez spoke seriously of what he considered a foolishness of Richard's.

"You must convince him. He should charge for his information and prescriptions. Our people do not expect anything valuable to be free. If the advice and treatment don't cost money, it is no good. The farmers listen to him but they do not follow his advice. This thing breaks Richard's heart."

Dr. Ramírez sighed. "During the past month five farmers have come from his site to see me. They know they will have to pay a fee but they want my advice. When I prescribe the same drugs and treatment Richard has advised, they are angry. They want something different and better because my advice is costing money. It is a great difficulty."

Richard came back to the table as the waiter appeared with our lunch.

A steak platter serving of bite-sized fried pork skins, salted almost white, was brought to each of us. Another plate held pickles, cubes of green tomatoes, and celery. One morsel of the meat required a swallow of beer to wash it down. Even with the beer I was certain my stomach was awash with brine.

While we ate, Richard bounced up and down, dancing first with one girl and then the other The meal must have occupied the better part of two hours and six bottles of beer for each man.

After my third bottle of beer I refused but the men continued to reorder without any apparent effect. It may have been that I was, by that time, in no condition to judge. After three beers life had assumed a rhapsodic quality.

The beer spawned a new idea. Dr. Ramírez would drive us to Pereira where I was to catch the feeder plane. After the men drank a final bottle for the road we climbed into the jeep again for a ride I didn't expect to enjoy.

The doctor's driving was unbelievably efficient! He zipped along, observing all road signs, staying in his lane, and conducting a running conversation at the same time. Richard's answers were equally as prompt. Once, when the doctor inquired if my silence meant I wasn't interested in their conversation, they both laughed at Richard's explanation that I didn't hold my liquor very well.

Dr. Ramírez cut a sizeable chunk off the time it had taken us to travel the same distance by bus. We were coming into Pereira when he again referred to Richard's disturbing refusal to charge fees. He repeated the story of the five farmers. Richard's face tightened.

"Who were they?"

The doctor recited the names.

"Yes, I did prescribe for them." He sounded dejected.

"If you would charge you could change that. They would respect your advice and you could belong to the club too. At least you'd have someplace to go other than those filthy holes in Mistrató for entertainment."

"I know." Richard didn't argue.

"One more thing. I have told you many times but you do not learn. One cannot die with each animal he loses. Each time you lose an animal you plunge a knife in your heart." The doctor raised one hand from the wheel, lifted his fist in the air and dramatically lowered it to thump against his chest. "It is an over-affliction of conscience."

"But so often it is the only valuable possession the family has," Richard objected mildly.

"It makes no difference. Your own people have a saying for it." He switched to heavily accented English. "One cannot gain everything."

Richard looked puzzled and then laughed.

"You mean 'You can't win 'em all.' "

"Yes, yes." The doctor repeated the phrase in English and then returning to Spanish added, "I'm telling the farmers to consult you. I say if the gringo can't cure it, I can't either."

"That's not true." Richard's voice was flat.

"It's almost true. Anything you do not understand you come running to me. You should get money for all the trouble and trips you make."

The doctor was still belaboring the point when he stopped in front of a hotel. But when the luggage was set on the sidewalk he abandoned his persuasion and the men shook hands and hugged each other, almost as if an older brother was parting from a favored younger one. Then the doctor turned to me and bid me a heel-clicking farewell.

As we rode up in the hotel elevator I asked if Richard knew the farmers who had consulted the doctor.

"I know them. All big farmers. They can afford to run around checking up on my advice. I'm not really here to help them."

The bellboy carried our bags into the room and left.

"I'm not supposed to charge for my work. That's what the Peace Corps is all about. Maybe I do convince only one farmer in ten, but he's the guy I'm here to help."

He sat on the bed, his clasped hands hanging loosely between his knees. He seemed to be brooding over Dr. Ramírez's dismal view of his struggles.

Beyond the bed was an open door, exposing a charming sight! A fully-equipped, white porcelain bathroom! As the tub filled I hung out fresh garments, knowing they too were probably infested with bedbugs. When I sank into the hot water it was the realization of a dream. My soaking took so long that when I came out of the bathroom Richard was asleep.

Of course all that beer could have had something to do with it! I climbed into a bed which had springs and a bugless mattress when it was barely dusk. As I luxuriated in the clean comfort I knew my 'enduring' was over. Strangely enough I regretted I hadn't been able to stay longer.

If I'd had more time maybe I could have begun a few small improvements for the women of Mistrató. The first third of my visit I'd walked around in a fog, trying to adjust to the obstacles of mere survival; the next five days were wasted while I learned the 'whys' of many things. It was only during the last third of my stay that any hint of inspiration arrived.

But it was too late now! Tomorrow I would fly back to the States.

18
Sunday in Pereira

The rising sun, streaming through the single uncurtained window and bouncing dazzling light off white walls wakened me. Richard's bed was empty. Although we were on the 7th floor the hum of street traffic below announced that Pereira was already awake and busy. From the open window one could see the Plaza and the four streets bordering it.

Below, men riding bicycles were zipping along, the upper portions of their bodies obscured by immense trays of bread balanced on their heads. Other riders transported trays of avocados and tomatoes. A couple rode by on a motor bike, the boy dressed in a business suit and the girl inspecting nylon-clad legs as she rode side-saddle behind him. They dismounted in front of the church. The

EIGHTEEN

Plaza walks were clogged with people, also heading for the church. As the church bells pealed out, the clock in its steeple pointed to six. Sunday started early in Pereira.

Behind me the shower shut off in the bathroom and in a few minutes Richard came out, rubbing traces of shaving cream from his face.

"We'd better eat first and then go to the airline office and confirm your reservations."

"I thought you confirmed them before we left Mistrató."

"I sent a telegram." Then seeing no comprehension he added, "The telegraph service here is like a lot of other things. Sometimes it works and sometimes it doesn't."

He got a clean shirt out of his bag.

"I'll go down and find out when the restaurant opens while you're dressing." He finished buttoning his shirt and then clicked the door shut behind him, leaving me to another delightful tub bath. I was stepping into my dress when he returned.

"The restaurant's open now. I had a cup of coffee and it's pretty good."

After a hasty glance in the mirror, which I hoped couldn't be a good reflection, I followed him out.

The elevator boy this morning wasn't more than ten years old but we got in anyway. He stopped it smoothly at the ground floor. A moment later we were scanning the menu in the coffee shop.

"Oh, they have our kind of breakfasts," I said. Richard gave me a glance of amusement. When our plates arrived I saw why.

The fried eggs were swimming in yellow oil. Two limp, rubbery strips of bacon had expired beside them. The toast was thick, pale, toasted only on one side, and the other side was slathered with the same yellow oil which dripped off onto the cold china and congealed. Although the food was tasteless I ate anyway, not because I was hungry but because I needed nourishment.

When we finished we went outside to the street. Most of the stores were opening. We passed everyone on the sidewalks as we barged along the three blocks to the airline office. The airline office wasn't open yet so we window-shopped until a man arrived with a key.

When Richard presented my ticket a minor hassle occurred.

"We know nothing about this ticket," the young man told Richard, offering it back to him as if that closed the matter.

"I wired two days ago," Richard said. He didn't accept the ticket.

"Telegraph difficulties are not our concern." The man gave my ticket a little shove, leaving it a few inches closer to Richard. My son put his hands in his pockets.

There were several minutes of rapid Spanish and I could tell from Richard's tone he was controlling his temper. At this point another young man arrived who joined them. The two employees consulted with each other. Richard turned to me, rolling his eyes heavenward.

"They didn't get my telegram and they say now they can't confirm your reservation. They want you to buy a new ticket for a later date."

EIGHTEEN

A few weeks ago such information would have thrown me into a tizzy, but now I had lived in Colombia half a month. It seemed I would be here slightly longer than I planned. While we waited, a third person arrived and climbed into an office set several feet above the other two cubicles. The consulting pair immediately presented the problem to the latest arrival. He took the ticket and came at once to talk with Richard.

There was the customary handshaking and back-slapping before he and Richard began to discuss my ticket. This man was not flustered by our difficulty and after a short explanation he nodded. Richard left my ticket with him and came back to tell me there would be a two-hour delay. As we walked outside I asked the reason.

"They have to phone Bogotá."

"But does it take two hours? Why don't they call now?"

Richard laughed. "Now, Mother, that's not the way things are done here. They have to do the courtesy bit with the telephone operator here and then with every connecting operator clear down through the airline office in Bogotá before they reach the right person. It all takes time."

A recollection of my single call to Colombia during the previous year came back to me. The connection had been poor and the inquiries by the Bogotá operator as to my health and family had raised my blood pressure to an explosive level while I counted the cost per minute of such chit-chat! However, when the bill arrived the phone company had not charged for the minutes used by courtesies.

We'd been trotting in the general direction of the hotel when we passed a beauty shop sign on a corner.

"Where is that beauty shop?" Maybe that dust mop I'd seen in the mirror this morning could be renovated.

Richard stopped and looked around. Then he backed to the curb, looking up.

"There," he pointed to a tiny balcony overlooking the street.

"Where's the door?"

He walked around the corner and stopped beside a door flush with the street. Beside it was a tiny circle barely big enough for a fingertip. "That's the doorbell. When you push it they release a catch upstairs and the door will open."

"Could I walk in without an appointment and get my hair done?"

"Probably. Go up and ask them. I have a couple of errands so I'll take care of them."

He walked on as soon as the door clicked open. I mounted a flight of stairs while a naked baby peered down at my progress. At the top was a short hall, leading to an apartment, the open doors revealing the rooms. Following the sound of conversation I went to the first door.

Inside was a modern beauty shop fronting on the balcony. Two women were in the chairs and the operators were teasing long, heavy black hair into towering hairdos. One lady, whose hair was waist length, was having it piled nearly a foot above her forehead in the most intricate combination of rolls and curlicues I'd ever seen. While I waited, the operator completed the style and sprayed a fog of mist over the skyscraper of undulations.

When the customer turned her head to view the back in a hand mirror, the edifice didn't even wobble. As the lady with the skyscraper left, the operator turned to me.

"Can you do my hair?"

"When?"

"Now."

"Why not?" She consulted her wristwatch. "What do you want done?"

"Shampoo and set." I glanced about the room and saw no shampoo basins, only the lavatory.

The lavatory turned out to be where my hair was washed. When I was doubled over far enough to reach the Colombian-height basin I felt as if I were standing on my head. My operator was energetic. She sudsed with gusto. Her vigorous scrubbing would have left my hair clean if I'd had five times as much. She set it on rollers and put me under a dryer which had no temperature setting. When I'd broiled sufficiently she took me out to comb.

Colombian women must have tough scalps. While the operator teased, tears ran down my face. If she noticed my discomfort, she ignored it. When my hair was frizzed into a cottony mass she sprayed the vanilla scented mist over it in a choking fog. Then she disappeared into the back of the house and from the sounds I heard I think she was doing her dishes.

After a while she reappeared and began brushing my hair into some semblance of the hair style I'd drawn on an envelope, with her own original additions. As the cork-screws mounted and climbed I discarded my intention to wear a hat on my return trip. No hat would perch on top of this creation without looking like the cherry on a sundae.

Richard was waiting at the hotel and when he saw me he began to smile.

"You look like a Colombian. What do you do about your hair at night?"

"I don't know. Maybe you hang your head on the bedpost."

He chuckled a little at my over-ornamentation before he gave me the news.

"I went back to the airline office, too. The schedule has been changed and your plane doesn't leave Bogotá until tomorrow."

"What about the connection in Mexico City?"

"Same thing."

In the original reservation my date of leaving had been changed twice. Mexico and Colombia had shifted from the Monday, Wednesday, Friday schedule to the alternate three days, fortunately in unison. Within a week I was notified they had returned to the original three days. Now, in the space of fifteen more days, they'd changed their minds once more.

"So now what do we do?"

"I'll show you the sights. You've got to see the statue."

A few people in Mistrató, those who had been as far away as Pereira, had mentioned a statue. Their expressions told me they thought the sculpture a disgrace to Colombia. When Richard took me to the center of the Plaza to see the statue their distaste was understandable.

The gigantic statue was at least four times life-size.

Mounted on a rearing horse of magnificent proportions was a nude man with long streaming hair, whose face was fierce with wild, blank eyes.

"Bolívar," Richard said. Then followed a short history of the event which led to the sculpting of this monument. "He's the country's hero but most of the peasants think he's been disgraced by nakedness."

We trotted across the Plaza and down a side street where Richard stopped at a small shop jammed with people crowding up to a counter behind which electric shake mixers whirred busily. Above the heads of the waitresses was a list of twenty-two items.

"All drinks, fruit or vegetable," Richard explained. He translated aloud. "Apple, banana, blackberry, cherry, corn, cherimoya, onion, bean, okra, tomato, orange, guava, mango, papaya, and some others we don't have words for."

The waitress presented a glass of lavender foamy liquid to the man in front of me.

"I'll have that," I decided.

"A blackberry and a tomato," Richard ordered.

The waitress dropped two ripe tomatoes into a mixer and pressed the switch. In the other she dumped a small can of blackberries. After only a few seconds she poured our drinks through strainers into glasses.

The drinks were as delicious as they had looked. I sampled Richard's and was surprised at the difference in taste between the canned juice at home and the fresh juice.

As we sipped I asked, "Don't they sell anything here except drinks?"

"No, and this is the first place any Peace Corps worker coming through town visits." As he drained his glass he glanced at the clock on the wall. "Say, we've got time for you to see the church."

I expected to walk back to the Plaza but Richard hailed a taxi and we were taken to the airport where we climbed on a rickety plane and almost immediately after we were airborne the plane landed again at another airport in a town forty miles away. A short trip by cab took us to a huge cathedral. The entry way was a gagging assortment of smells—disinfectant, garlic, spices, and urine.

The sanctuary was a domed structure rising three floors to a ceiling whose entire surface was covered with murals. We tiptoed inside and stood behind a group of people crowding against the last pew. Richard leaned his head near my ear and whispered.

"Look at that painting on the left, near the ceiling."

It was a picture of Christ with a disciple kneeling in front of him. The view showed the upper three-fourths of their figures with an odd exception. Where the oval frame bound the painting on the lower right, the artist had left the shin and foot of the kneeling disciple to the imagination. Either he, or a later artist had corrected the omission. A plaster leg and foot had been added, extending over the top of the frame and some eighteen inches below.

"See, his foot and leg are hanging out."

It was a fascinating innovation!

My eyes dropped to the congregation. Unlike stateside congregations there was no uniformity of dress. Women dressed in unmistakably expensive clothes sat beside others in threadbare housedresses. Beggars in tatters knelt beside men in silk suits. All heads moved forward or backward as they knelt or sat in rhythm with the service. The priest at the front seemed to be doing several things at once.

To the left of the altar on a wheeled funeral cart was a casket. Surrounding it were so many black-clad women and men that the dark polished wood was nearly hidden.

In the center of the church people filled the communion rail in a solid, wriggling line.

On the right stood a couple, the girl in a white wedding dress. The pair waited at motionless attention while the rest of the wedding party behind them shifted restlessly. The priest finished giving communion and the rail emptied, refilling again immediately, but he moved over to the casket.

The altar boys followed, swinging incense and ringing a small bell. A funeral service was begun and then abruptly stopped as the priest crossed to the wedding party. He conducted the marriage ceremony to the point where the couple knelt and a lady in the wedding party threw a white, silken rope over the couple's shoulders. At this juncture he returned to the replacements waiting at the communion rail.

I raised my eyebrows questioningly at Richard and he mouthed a word.

"Later."

We watched the priest go through another section of all three rituals before we left. When we climbed into the waiting cab I was full of questions.

"Why is he doing all those different things at once?"

"So the wedding party and the funeral will have good attendance. He sets these personal services to coincide with mass."

"Does he do this every Sunday?"

"Sometimes more than once. He says three masses and if enough people have died or want to get married he may have a funeral and wedding at each service."

"It's very confusing." There had been an unsettling similarity to a three-ring circus.

"Not to them. It's reassuring. When a poor person dies or a peasant girl gets married the family knows just as many people will attend the service as if they were wealthy."

We rode a few blocks in silence. Some of the new values I'd acquired on this trip were churning around in my head. The single time I'd understood something Richard had missed was a case in point.

A Volunteer stationed on a remote site had become violently ill with infestation. The most intelligent local farmer had been dispatched to the nearest town with a phone to alert the Peace Corps doctor. In the interim, before the doctor arrived, the local witch doctor who was the nearest thing the town had to a medical man, brought a group of people and led a lengthy ceremony outside the Volunteer's house. His trips to the privy, sometimes in time and sometimes too late, were witnessed by the assemblage who were going through a weird combination of incantations and hymns. He told Richard, "I thought I was dying and all these lunatics were standing around watching me and doing that mish-mash." In his agony he'd lived a nightmare.

"But they gave him all the help they had," I objected. "What more could they do?"

Richard had been startled. "I never thought of it that way. They gave him the best they had to offer. That's total involvement!"

The taxi turned a corner and pulled up in front of a solid wall of doors. Richard opened the taxi door.

"Mary and Helen, two girl Volunteers live here. I'm going to see if anyone is home and maybe we can make plans for this evening." He got out of the cab and punched a doorbell. The door clicked and he disappeared inside. A few minutes later he returned.

"Mary's invited us to eat supper with them. There are some other Volunteers in town and they'll be over this evening," he said as he reentered the cab.

A scowl spread over his face. "I want you to do something for me. Mary's mother is here. Will you entertain her for a couple of hours so we can go out to a bar?"

"Entertain her? How?"

"Just visiting. She came in the same day you did."

"Did she come on the same flight?"

"Nope, she came out of New York. She'll be here two more weeks." He turned to face me. "I want you to promise me something. Tell me you won't argue with her."

"Argue!" My disposition must be worse than I thought. "Of course I won't."

A peculiar expression flickered across his face. "She may not be exactly what you expect."

His words were slightly intimidating. Maybe Mrs. Smith was someone very special. But no matter, with the common ground of our visits it would be an interesting evening.

"There are other things you ought to see in this town," Richard said and we were off at a run on another jaunt.

He dragged me through the local market, another church, a trip by cable car to the top of a mountain where we ambled through a shrine and ate in the concession beside it. There was little talk between us. Richard kept up a running commentary and I gasped for breath. When I thought I would drop with exhaustion he located another taxi and we rode back to Mary's apartment. When we entered she was waiting at the top of the stairs.

Mary Smith, which is not her name, was a short, plump girl with a neat ponytail on either side of her head. She had a freshly scrubbed appearance and the gathered print skirt and white blouse she wore became her although the garments had seen better days. Richard introduced us and as we went into her living room I caught a glimpse of electric appliances in her kitchen. The living room was colorful with native furniture, bright serapes, and local art. While I was admiring her ingenuity, footsteps sounded in the hall.

"Mother, I'd like for you to know Mrs. Smith."

Mrs. Smith was an average, middle-aged woman with greying hair and glasses. She was dressed in a neat cotton and oxfords.

"I'm glad to see someone from home," she said as she

came into the living room. "I don't have to ask you if you are having a good time. This is the end of the earth, isn't it?"

I laughed, and almost as if it was a signal Mary and Richard vanished into the kitchen. While Mrs. Smith and I were still filling each other in on homes in the United States the two young people left the apartment to shop for supper.

"That's the way it is," Mrs. Smith said, as the door closed behind them. "Mary pays no attention to me but runs all over this filthy town doing God knows what! If the trip hadn't been so expensive I'd go right back home. What airline did you take down? You flew, didn't you?"

"Yes." I related an abbreviated version of my trip.

"You should have come out of New York. I flew only seven hours."

"But I live 2,000 miles from New York."

Mrs. Smith gave me her full, curious attention. "But you've been to New York, haven't you?"

I shook my head.

Her curiosity changed to horror. "My God, never been to New York!"

I'd become an instant phenomenon. But I was the only one here from the States so she decided to make the best of it.

"What kind of a place did Richard have to live?"

I described Richard's house.

"You didn't stay in that hole, did you?"

"Yes. It took me a few days to get used to it though."

"You should have made him get you a better place.

One thing you have to learn right away and that is how to deal with these people."

"What do you mean?"

"At first they came up to me and pawed me."

"Pawed you?"

"Put their hands on me, felt my clothing, even wanted to touch my skin. Everytime I went out I had to take another bath when I came home."

There seemed no need to expose my own carelessness, touching and being touched each time I went to town without a second thought. My standards of cleanliness had shifted downward.

"How did you stop their wanting to touch you?"

"I slapped their hands away. Then when they tried to jabber at me in that stupid lingo they talk I told them loud and clear to speak English, the civilized language."

I suppressed a shudder, imagining the pained surprise such treatment would have caused Doña Albertina. There would have been lowered lashes to conceal sudden tears. I took a deep breath and the adrenalin from my anger jolted me as I opened my mouth.

Then I closed it again, letting the air out slowly. I'd made a promise. I made no comment. Mrs. Smith didn't need any. She launched into a tirade about the foolish altruism which misled her daughter into joining the Peace Corps. The poverty-stricken barrios which Mary visited were described although Mrs. Smith had only driven past. Mrs. Smith equated poverty with dirt. A particular complaint was the night course her daughter was giving the inmates of the jail. Mrs. Smith pointed to some delicately fashioned plastic flowers on the coffee table and was telling me they were a gift of the prisoners when Mary and Richard returned.

"Why, those flowers aren't worth ten cents," Mrs. Smith spat.

The young people caught her last words. I gave Richard a hard look as Mrs. Smith looked away for a moment. He grinned, raising his eyebrows and shoulders at the same time behind the woman's back, in perfect awareness my boiling point had been reached and controlled.

Mary got the message too but when I took a second look at her face I was sorry I glared. Her eyes were red and swollen. Richard's willingness to expose me to this flood of vitriol was evidence that the girl was almost at the breaking point.

The pair took their groceries into the kitchen and began to prepare supper. A few moments later they called us. Helen, Mary's roommate was not expected for the meal. Helen, it appeared, had been absent a great deal more than usual lately.

"Where did you get this ham?" I inquired as I helped myself to a slice to lay over the cheese on my sandwich.

"There's one store in town that stocks food like this but we can't afford to buy there very often," Mary answered. "Look, our kind of coffee and condensed milk too." She held up a small jar of instant coffee and a small can of milk.

"Tonight we're Little America," Richard judged.

Mary smiled, and with the anxiety gone she was pretty.

The food was excellent and the coffee hot and savory. I lingered over my second cup, ashamed to lower the crystals in the expensive little glass jar any further by my greediness. When we were finished I offered to help with the dishes.

"Oh, no, you're company," Richard said, urging Mrs. Smith and me back into the living room. "You mothers take it easy."

Translation—"Go in the other room and listen so Mary can have peace a little longer."

Mrs. Smith picked up her invective where she'd left off. I heard about the wisdom of living in New York as compared to the ignorance of living in the boondocks of Texas. I was confided the secret that some of Mary's American girl friends here were no better than they should be, whatever that meant. As the minutes dragged by I made a delightful discovery.

I could nod and smile whenever the words lagged and not listen at all. Months later I was informed this course had resulted in my agreeing to a number of wild statements. By silence I had consented to all sorts of paranoic notions.

Mary and Richard lingered in the kitchen until Helen and the other Volunteers arrived. The conversation was caught up and carried away among them, each reporting on his own project or latest debacle. Their conversation was serious except for one report which was an occasion for amusement.

Helen pulled up her dress, displaying a large bruise a few inches above the back of her knee.

"Today, on a crowded bus," she explained.

"But that's not where they pinch me," Mary objected.

Helen smiled. "Not you, maybe, because you're short. But I'm five feet ten inches tall and when I'm standing among Colombians that's where their hands hit me."

There was a general discussion about the mistake Mary had made the first time someone pinched her. She had not known it was meant to be a compliment from an unknown admirer.

"I screamed," she giggled, "and everyone on the bus stared at me as if I'd done something naughty. It scared me a little and for a while I took taxis but it was too expensive, so now when I feel a hand snaking around for a pinch I begin wiggling in the opposite direction. I still get a few though," she concluded ruefully.

The girls took the hazard in good spirits but Mrs. Smith leaned toward me and hissed, "I told you these people were no better than animals."

Instantly every young face in the room took on a poker-faced expression in the silence that followed her remark. Then one of the boys rose.

"Let's go down to the bar. Would you like to come, Mrs. Sanders?" The exclusion was embarrassingly obvious.

"No, she wouldn't," Richard answered hastily. "The mothers are enjoying a visit."

As the young people trooped out I got an oblique look and half-smile from Helen. But Mrs. Smith was glad to have a captive listener and during their absence she regaled me with comments from a tongue dripping acid.

On the flight back to Pereira Richard apologized.

"I knew what you were in for. Mary told me this afternoon how it was but her mother is driving her crazy and I thought you could stand it for a few hours."

I wanted to ask if I'd sounded like Mrs. Smith when I arrived but lacked the courage.

"What does Mrs. Smith do during the day?"

"Nothing. That's the trouble. She won't go out on the street if she can help it. She doesn't want the dirty people to touch her."

"She missed complaining about the streetwalkers. I thought she'd be livid on that subject."

"She doesn't know about them. Mary never told her who all those women were."

For some reason I found the picture of Mrs. Smith rubbing elbows with the pathetic victims of the street most gratifying. Spitefully I hoped that some day Mary would tell her.

"Hasn't Mary taken her mother anywhere?"

"The tourist attractions. She can't let her mother meet any of the people she's working with. One incident of slapping hands or shouting by her mother and Mary might as well pack up and go home."

He'd given me the answer to my unspoken question. After plopping me down in the center of his people, he'd gone away on his own affairs. My elation amounted to euphoria!

"Did Mary send her mother any of the literature you sent me?"

"Yeah, nearly all of it, but I guess you noticed that if

it isn't happening in New York it's hardly worth mentioning at all. The rest of the world is wilderness."

"Including Texas," I laughed.

"Especially Texas," Richard guffawed. "My boots proved it to her."

When we turned out the light that night, snuggling again in the soft clean beds, I reviewed my own behavior in Mistrató. Had I said or done anything which would jeopardize Richard's work in the future? I hoped not!

The last thing I remember before I fell asleep was thinking that it would be a blessing when Mrs. Smith returned to her oasis of perfection. In the meantime, Mary was sentenced to listen to her mother for two more punishing weeks!

19
Too Much Too Fast

"And as we leave this land of tropical splendor," an unctuous travelogue voice intoned in my head as I boarded the plane at Pereira. Those regretful syllables always signalled the retreat from whatever land of enchantment you'd been pictorially visiting.

A travelogue picture of Mistrató would undoubtedly include shots of the cloud-capped mountains, the grandeur of their sheer drop to valley floors where foaming water rushed over ebony stones. There would be close-ups of giant avocados, huge stalks of plátano, and a panoramic view of coffee trees marching in neat lines up steep slopes. Shrines embedded in mountainsides, the witch-doctor's wares, or a group shot of women slapping their laundry on the rocks in the river might capture a flavor of quaintness. Nothing would hint that Mistrató was anything less than a secret paradise.

The photographer wouldn't include mudslides or boulders loosened by rain and periodically obliterating the narrow twisting roads. No film would be devoted to the limited food supply in the groceries nor the selection of meat displayed on market day. The walking somnambulism of a population malnourished from birth would be missed, not even suspected, by a visiting filmmaker. The smiling faces and warm reception would belie such an intimation. But Mistrató was all these things too.

Mistrató was a backward flip from the springboard of modern Bogotá into Colombia's past, to an almost unreachable village still moving lethargically in traditional patterns, sequestered by poor roads, few vehicles, and a lack of television through which the people might be exposed to a changing world. The town could have stagnated forever except for the determination of a visionary few. The yeasty convolutions of progress had commenced several years ago. At least three people were striving before the Peace Corps was invited to help.

Padre Ortiz was already engaged in combat against ancient beliefs. Dr. Vallejo had brought his education and skills to assist. Mayor García had taken an objective look at the town. The upshot was the city fathers had requested a Peace Corps Volunteer and Richard appeared.

And into the somnolence of Mistrató tramped the gringo, ignoring the dictates of caste by working with his hands, preaching the necessity of cleanliness to a people comfortable with dirt, and persuading men to cooperate who formerly eyed each other with suspicion. During that initial year the people had become inured to his inexplicable demands and bizarre beliefs. And then the gringo brought his mother.

If the gringo was strange, his mother was even stranger. She wore gaudy clothing to bed. Although she'd lived an unbelievable half-century she lacked the dignity to age gracefully as did the women of Mistrató. She careened about town, her gait only slightly slower than the gringo's, asking for all sorts of unknown condiments. No grocery could supply her queer requests. It was clear to everyone she knew nothing about washing clothes. Altogether, she would be a trial and burden to any man. Such was the opinion of all but a few in Mistrató.

And my own opinion wasn't much higher. When Richard had asked if I wanted to visit Mistrató or make reservations in the nearest modern hotel where he would spend the time with me, I'd chosen his site. How could I know what his life was if I didn't see his home? There were no doubts in my mind. I was well prepared for the experience. The Peace Corps would have disagreed.

Their careful screening of applicants, the several months of intensive training, and the dozens of orientation lectures are no more than is needed by a Volunteer. The indoctrination carries the Volunteer through assimilation into an alien culture. In spite of the many-faceted preparation, so much suffering occurs in the process of acculturation that the misery has acquired a term. The Peace Corps calls it Culture Shock.

The collision with a foreign culture is an agitating

confrontation. No matter what words are used, a slight discrepancy exists between the printed term 'native medicines' and the sight of hogs in flannel neckties. If 'primitive' suggests a jolly camping-out, a visitor is immediately disabused of this notion as soon as the bedbugs commence to bite.

If one is an incurable optimist, watching an entrail consumed, a glueball of rice devoured, or a potato baked with *carne gratis* disappear down the gullet across the table should generate second thoughts.

The sun hadn't sunk slowly from the majesty of violet peaks to the sweet, exotic link of a tropical night as it should have in any self-respecting travelogue. No, the sun had blazed away in all its usual flash-bulb brilliance as my plane left the shores of Colombia. I hadn't left peace and tranquillity behind. A seething, predictable convulsion was even now rumbling in the hinterlands. No flower-scented mountain breeze was bringing blessed nighttime repose to Mistrató.

There was only an uneasy blackness which might be split by a shot as some enraged farmer attempted to delay the grassroots stirrings. As the plane flew over Mexico I tried to organize my impressions, the sights, the surprises.

My family would have questions. After their concern about Richard's welfare had been satisfied, they would ask if I enjoyed the trip. As the plane neared home, I still didn't know the answer.

The trip couldn't be described as fun, fun, fun! The worst deprivation I'd ever known was in Mistrató. But miserable wasn't the right word either. The friendships I'd left behind were doubly precious because they were so few. Was the trip a good rest? No one in his right mind would call it that. For the first few days I'd been felled by exhaustion. Amusing? Too glowing. Fruitful? Possibly. Devastating? No, given another week I'd have been challenging the environment with some solutions of my own.

My landing in Texas wasn't a proud moment. Decorated by a hair style which now resembled the leaning tower of Pisa, polka-dotted with bedbug bites, scaling from over-enthusiastic applications of bleach in the bathwater, and eight pounds thinner, I was a distressing surprise to my family, but they took me to their bosoms anyway.

And just as expected, when the urgencies of Richard's health and welfare had been answered, the query came.

"How was the trip? Did you have a good time?"

No words of my own could compress the tidal wave of experiences into a simple answer, so I used some of my son's.

"It was a blast, a real mind-blower."

Epilogue

During the year following my trip, I tried to carry
out the promises made in Mistrató. Back in Texas, I talked
of the destitution in the little town and offers came to
help. A local sewing machine repairman searched his
catalogs for the model owned by Doña Albertina. It
proved to be an obsolete model with no parts or needles
available. We selected an assortment of needles and sent
them to Father Ortiz. The last I heard was that the patient priest had ground them all down into usable sizes!

Six months after my return, Richard sent pictures of
school gardens burgeoning with produce, albeit planted
in drunken rows. Mr. Walter Baxter, a Weslaco seed man,
had donated the seeds for Richard's project; his gift had
produced giant vegetables on the slopes of the Andes—
including five-pound turnips. Mr. Baxter's detailed instructions about gathering seed from the crop insured
the schools of future crops after Richard's departure.

The attempts to get assistance for Dr. Vallejo met with apparent success. Miss Jacquelyne McAdams brought the matter before her chapter of Sigma Alpha Iota, the sorority of professional musicians, and the group enlisted the help of a medical man. More than a ton of discarded medical equipment, drug and toothpaste samples, and medical reference books was collected. Enthusiasm for the project spread and the Brazoria County Medical Auxiliary offered to supply more samples and package the shipment.

A collection of this size would require a legal permit to enter Colombia. Miss McAdams, working through CARE authorities in Dallas, was able to clear it for shipment from the States. But Richard, working through channels in Colombia, could get no written consent.

Months of frustrating effort went into trying to get permission for the shipment's legal entry. Letters, phone calls, and personal visits to Colombian officials met with many promises but no action. When an answer finally came, it was a refusal. Several more months passed before Richard could trace the reason.

He had made a protocol mistake and neglected a minor bureaucrat over whose desk the permit would pass in its travels through coordinating offices. No amount of soothing or apologies could persuade the man to rescind his objection. He was determined to make his authority felt. The result was that Dr. Vallejo remained without a minimum of equipment and the donations rotted in a Texas junkyard.

When Richard's two years in Mistrató were finished,

the town gave him a party. Even the poorest took part in the fiesta and a few people told him they understood what he'd tried to do. Richard must have been overcome by their gratitude; instead of coming home, he signed up for an extra year. Working as part of the Peace Corps staff, he was *papacita* to 46 Volunteers and liaison between them and the Colombian government.

During his year on the staff, Richard and Volunteers John Thomas and Robert Trafford wrote an instruction pamphlet, complete with diagrams, entitled "How To Plow With a Mule." The Colombian government was so pleased with its clarity they printed it and distributed it through their own agencies. But Richard's heart lay in Mistrató. From time to time, he returned to the town, threading his way through the maze of transport, to spend time with old friends.

He returned to the States, graduated from college in 1970, and married a remarkable young lady, well-adapted to surviving Richard's crusading brainstorms. My life changed too, beginning with the recognition that my own tunnel vision was distressingly similar to the apathetic assumptions of Mistratóans. Looking around me, I saw more similarities.

When Mayor García complained that his town moved slowly against decades of custom and superstition, I had only to look up to see vitriolic controversy bubbling over everything from guitar music in church to women's rights, from hair lengths to horse-racing. Dr. Ramirez might have been describing my town where he said people don't expect anything of value to be free. The location of a free mobile X-ray unit in the poorer section of our town brought surprisingly little response. Investigation revealed that people thought the unit near them was inferior to the one provided for persons living in more affluent neighborhoods, although the two units were identical.

The Peace Corps, we know, has changed the lives of Volunteers. Sometimes it has even affected those it was intended to serve. It doesn't deal in miracles. And I don't think it ever contemplated the subject of Volunteers' mothers. . . .

Curiosity and maternal concern prompted my trip to Colombia but I expected to be a witness. Richard assumed I would participate. The trip was to be a hiatus. It was probably the most strenuous fifteen days of my life and permanently dislocated my point of view.

Richard had always been disappointed whenever I'd been slow to enter into any of his enthusiasms. In his youthful optimism, he had neglected to consider the possibility that I might be unable to adapt. In this case, perhaps, I justified his confidence that I would survive the galloping tours, the battering emotional jolts, and the tragically brave hopelessness of my new friends in Mistrató. That, itself, was a miracle of sorts.

[Publisher's postscript: Following a stint in the Army, Richard returned to Texas. He lives now in Big Spring with his wife and two children, and is employed at a federal correctional facility. The author died in 1978.]